The Hardy Boys®
in
The Sinister Signpost

This Armada book belongs to:

_____

_____

_____

Hardy Boys® Mystery Stories in Armada

For contractual reasons, Armada has been obliged to publish from No. 57 onwards before publishing Nos. 49–56. These missing numbers will be published as soon as possible.

The Hardy Boys® Mystery Stories

The Sinister Signpost

Franklin W. Dixon

ARMADA

First published in the U.K. in 1972 by
William Collins Sons & Co. Ltd, London and Glasgow
First published in Armada in 1975
This impression 1989

Armada is an imprint of
the Children's Division, part of
the Collins Publishing Group,
8 Grafton Street, London W1X 3LA

Printed and bound in Great Britain by
William Collins Sons & Co. Ltd, Glasgow

Tadlow jumped to his feet and whirled round to face the Hardys

CONTENTS

·1·

Danger on Wheels

"Do you see what I see?" Joe Hardy asked his brother.

"It's a dragster," Frank replied. "They're not supposed to be driven on public roads. At least not in this state."

The Hardys were driving home from Taylorville along Shore Road in their open convertible. It was a sunny, summer afternoon. So far, they had encountered almost no traffic. Now Frank was gaining on the slow-moving, bright-orange racing car. In the driver's seat, situated aft of the car's massive rear wheels, sat a helmeted, black-jacketed figure.

"He's sure travelling at low speed," Joe remarked. "I wonder why."

Frank, dark-haired and eighteen, accelerated and attempted to pass the other vehicle. The driver of the dragster increased his own speed and prevented the convertible from going by.

"What's he trying to do? Cause an accident?" Joe said angrily.

Frank was forced to return to his position behind the dragster. As he did so, the driver again reduced speed to a snail's pace.

Blond-haired Joe, who was a year younger and

more impetuous than Frank, stood up and cupped his hands over his mouth. "Okay!" he shouted at the other driver. "You've had your fun! Now let us by!"

Frank made another attempt to pass. Suddenly the driver of the dragster manœuvred his vehicle in such a way that its left rear wheel slammed up against the right front wheel of the Hardys' car.

"We're out of control!" Joe yelled.

Their car swerved violently as a result of the impact. Frank struggled with the steering wheel and managed to regain control. He quickly came to a stop. The boys watched as the dragster sped down the road out of sight.

"I'd like to get my hands on that clown!" Joe said, fuming.

"So would I," Frank agreed. "But the dragster had no licence plates. We'd have a hard time trying to track down the car."

The boys inspected the damage to their convertible. The right front bumper was crumpled and the rim of the wheel badly bent.

"We'd better replace the wheel with our spare," Frank suggested.

The Hardys jacked up the car. While they worked, a large, open truck approached on the opposite side of the road. As it flashed by, Joe caught a glimpse of a bright-orange dragster in the rear of the vehicle.

"Look!" he exclaimed. "That must be the same racing car that rammed us!"

Frank jumped to his feet and peered in the direction his brother was pointing. By now the speeding truck had vanished round a bend in the road.

"Everything happened so fast," Joe said disappointedly, "I wasn't able to get the licence number of the truck."

"Too bad," Frank commented. "It'll be miles away by the time we finish putting on the spare."

When the job was completed, the boys continued their journey home. Mrs Hardy, a slim, graceful woman, greeted them when they arrived.

"I'm so glad you're back," she announced. "Your father wants to see you right away."

The boys sprinted up the stairs to their father's study on the second floor. Mr Hardy, a distinguished-looking, middle-aged man, was seated behind his desk.

"Hi, Dad!" Joe greeted him. "Mother said you wanted to see us."

"Hello, boys," he replied. "I just accepted a new case that I'd like to discuss with you two."

Frank and Joe glanced at each other excitedly. Then they took seats near Mr Hardy's desk. He sat quietly for a moment, studying a myriad of notes he had spread out in front of him.

Fenton Hardy was an extremely meticulous man. Formerly a member of the New York City Police Department, he now worked as a private detective. His exceptional skill in solving baffling crimes had made him famous. In fact, many of his methods were studied and adopted by law-enforcement agencies throughout the world. Frank and Joe had inherited their father's talent, and often assisted him with his cases.

"Yes," Mr Hardy said finally, as he glanced up from his notes. "I believe we're in for a challenging case."

"We?" Joe exclaimed. "Did you say—we?"

Their father smiled. Although in his mid-forties, he appeared much younger than his years. "That's right," he assured his sons. "I'm going to need your help."

"That's great!" Frank declared. "What kind of case is it?"

Mr Hardy leaned back in his chair. "Have you ever heard of the Alden Automotive Research and Development Company?"

"Yes," Joe answered quickly. "It's a firm just a few miles south of Clayton. I believe they experiment with high-speed cars."

"Correct," the detective replied. "The company makes components for regular stock cars as well. Also—"

"Isn't Keith Alden the president of the company?" Frank interrupted. "I remember reading about him in the newspapers. He was once a famous racing driver."

"That's right," Mr Hardy replied.

He went on to tell his sons Alden had designed an experimental turbine motor for his high-speed racing cars.

"The power plant is so revolutionary that the government has shown an interest in it. However," the detective continued, "despite his efforts to keep the motor a secret, Mr Alden suspects that someone has learned about it and is trying to steal the plans."

"Does he have any idea who the person is?" Joe asked.

"None," his father replied. "And here's something else. Two of his cars, in which the motor was installed, met with accidents of a very mysterious nature."

Mr Hardy stated that Alden wanted to put his motor and car designs to a real test by entering them in road race competitions. "It was during test runs that the vehicles were totally destroyed. The drivers barely escaped with their lives."

"What happened?" Joe asked.

"The windshields of the cars suddenly crazed," he said, "and cut off the drivers' forward vision. As a result, they went out of control and crashed."

"Windshields crazed?" Joe muttered.

"Yes," Mr Hardy answered. "They turned almost a milky white."

"But how could that happen?" Frank asked.

"We don't know," his father admitted. "At first, Alden thought the windshields might have been made of a faulty material. But after a laboratory test, that theory proved to be wrong."

"What's our assignment, Dad?" Joe questioned eagerly.

Mr Hardy rose from his chair and slowly paced the floor. "I'm going to run a check on all of Alden's employees," he said. "That's just a matter of getting hold of the personnel files at the plant. However, such information seldom reveals the whole story about a man. I'd like to place as many of the workers as possible under close observation, especially the men in the research department."

"And you want Joe and me for an undercover job!" Frank exclaimed.

Their father grinned. "You're way ahead of me," he replied. "But you're right. It's exactly what I have in mind."

"That means we'll have to act as employees ourselves," Frank said. "The problem is how can we do it without arousing suspicion?"

"I have an idea," his brother answered. "Bayport High introduced a basic automotive engineering course last term. Suppose we say we want to work at the plant to get some practical experience."

"That's it," Frank said. "And the timing is perfect, since our school vacations have just started."

"Sounds good," Mr Hardy agreed. "You'll have a chance to meet Mr Alden tomorrow. He's permitting an automobile club to use his private race track for a dragster and a stock-car competition. We're invited to be his guests."

"Great!" Joe exclaimed. "Would it be all right to ask Chet to come along?"

"I don't see why not," his father replied.

Chet Morton was a school chum of the Hardys. He was a plump, good-natured boy, who lived with his family on a farm near Bayport.

Just then Mrs Hardy announced that supper was ready. The boys and their father were about to leave the study when an object crashed through one of the windows. It landed in a corner of the room.

"Get down!" Frank yelled.

A split second later there was a muffled explosion!

·2·

Threats

INSTANTLY the room was filled with thick, boiling clouds of smoke.

"What happened?" Joe shouted.

"It must have been a bomb!" Frank cried out.

The Hardys held their breaths and groped their way through the choking smoke. There was no sign of fire. Frank, Joe, and their father soaked handkerchiefs with water, held them over their faces, then began flinging open all the windows on the second floor. Gradually the smoke cleared.

"Eek!" they heard a woman scream. The boys turned to see the tall, angular form of their Aunt Gertrude rushing up the stairs, followed closely by Mrs Hardy.

"Everything's all right!" Frank announced, in an effort to calm the women.

"Smoke!" Aunt Gertrude cried. "Call the fire department! Call the police! Do something!"

"No need to get excited," Mr Hardy said. "There's no fire. Please go back downstairs. We'll explain everything later."

The boys dashed from the house to look for the thrower of the smoke bomb. Not finding him, the young detectives searched in a widening circle. Presently Frank noticed a small, glittering object some distance away. He ran to the spot and picked it up.

"Take a look at this!" he called to his brother.

"Why—it's a rifle cartridge case," Joe said, as he examined Frank's discovery.

"Let's show it to Dad."

The boys returned to their father's study. Mr Hardy was examining fragments of the bomb. He held up a metal tube about a foot long. "This is all that's left of what I'm certain was a rifle grenade."

Frank's eyes widened with astonishment. "A rifle grenade?" he echoed.

"Yes," Mr Hardy replied. "The explosive section is attached to one end of this tube. The other end fits over the muzzle of a rifle. It's then fired from the weapon by means of a blank cartridge shell."

"A shell like this?" Frank said, handing his father the cartridge case he had picked up.

An expression of surprise spread across the older detective's face. "Exactly!" he declared, studying the small object. "Where did you find this?"

"Just a few yards beyond our own grounds," Frank said. "That explains why we saw no footprints on our property."

Mr Hardy handed his sons a fragment of paper. "This was tied to the shaft of the smoke grenade," he told them.

Frank and Joe were amazed to find that it was a handwritten message which read:

You are being watched. Drop the Alden case, or the next smoke will be lethal!

"Leaping lizards!" Joe exclaimed. "We haven't even started on the case yet, and already we're being threatened!"

"This is something we can't ignore," Mr Hardy said. "We'll have to be extra cautious. And as for your mother and aunt, I'm going to ask them to take a little trip. We can't risk leaving them alone in the house."

During supper the two women rebuked the boys' father for suggesting that they go away.

"Would a sea captain be the first to leave his sinking ship?" Aunt Gertrude exclaimed. "Not on your life! I, for one, will not budge from this house!"

Mr Hardy's sister, unmarried, had a peppery temperament. She was always quick to express her opinions openly, and often made dire predictions about the horrible fate awaiting all detectives.

"We know you're concerned for our safety," Mrs Hardy added in her soft-spoken voice. "But we will not leave here."

"Well—all right," her husband conceded reluctantly. "However, I'm going to call Chief Collig at head-quarters and request that a couple of guards be posted near the house day and night."

The next day, Saturday, Mr Hardy and the boys had an early breakfast. Then, after driving to the Morton farm to pick up Chet, they headed for Alden's private race track near Clayton.

"I can't wait to see the stock-car competitions," Chet said, as he peeled a large banana. "In fact, I've been thinking of getting into the sport myself. There's an old car in my father's barn I'm planning to fix up."

"Oh-oh," Joe remarked jokingly. "That's one hobby you had better stay away from."

"Don't worry," Frank added with a laugh. "Chet's car will end up as a diner on wheels, rather than a threat to the racing world."

"Cut the small talk," their friend retorted. "You two master minds are jealous because I'm the daredevil type. We're a species that eat more because we need tons of energy."

The Hardys and Chet arrived at the track in less than an hour. The area was a beehive of activity. Bright-coloured stock cars and dragsters gleamed in the sun as drivers prepared their vehicles for the day's competitions.

"You fellows enjoy yourselves looking at some of these cars," Mr Hardy said. "I'll locate Mr Alden and bring him back here."

"Okay, Dad."

The boys began to stroll around the area. Suddenly Joe grabbed his brother's arm and exclaimed, "There's the dragster that rammed us!"

"It sure looks like it," Frank agreed. "Same colour. But let's not jump to conclusions. We'll ask the driver some questions first."

The Hardys and Chet walked towards the dragster. A slim, sandy-haired young man was working on the engine of the car.

"Are you the owner of this dragster?" Frank queried.

"Yeah," the young man sneered. "What's it to you?"

"Now hold on!" Joe interjected. "No need to get hot about it. He just asked a simple question."

"Were you driving along Shore Road in Bayport yesterday?" Frank continued.

The drag-strip racer hesitated for a moment. "Why don't you guys take a walk?" he shot back finally. "Especially the fat one with you. He looks like he could use some exercise."

"Who do you think you're talking to?" Chet snapped.

"Just a second," Joe said. He ran his hand round the outer surface of the vehicle's left rear wheel. "The wall of this tyre is roughed up. It must have rubbed hard against something."

"Such as our car!" Frank stated.

"Get away from that wheel!" the young man growled.

He gave Joe a shove that sent the boy crashing to the ground. Like a flash Joe was up on his feet. He rushed at his attacker and pinned his opponent's arms behind his back in a jujitsu manœuvre.

"Let me go!" the young man cried.

At that moment Mr Hardy appeared with Keith Alden. He was a tall, slim man with patrician features. His dark hair was slightly grey at the temples.

Mr Alden looked troubled. "What's going on here?" he demanded.

"Are you boys having trouble?" Mr Hardy asked quickly.

The car manufacturer spoke to Joe in a displeased voice. "Why are you holding on to my son like that?"

"Your—your son?" Frank stammered.

Joe released his grip on the young man.

"Yes," Alden continued. "This is my son Roger."

Mr Hardy introduced his client to the boys. Except for Roger, everyone was mutually embarrassed.

"These guys," the young man shouted, "are trying to pin some sort of car accident on me!"

Alden eyed Roger suspiciously. "I don't think the Hardy boys would accuse anyone without good reason. If you were involved in an accident, it wouldn't be the first time."

Frank and Joe glanced at each other. It seemed wise not to force the issue. They told Mr Alden about their encounter with a dragster the previous day, but could not say for certain that the driver of the bright orange car was Roger.

"Then only my son can clear up this matter," Alden said. He put the question to Roger.

The young man became even more arrogant. "I didn't ram into anybody's car, and I never heard of Shore Road!"

His father was in a quandary. Finally he said, "Until this matter can be investigated further, I forbid you to drive your dragster in the competitions today."

"We'll see about that!" Roger muttered defiantly. He glared at the Hardys, then turned and walked off at a furious pace.

"I don't know what to do about my son," Alden said with remorse. "His mother died several years ago, and I haven't been able to spend much time with him. He's been getting more difficult to live with every day."

"I'm sure he'll straighten out," Mr Hardy remarked sympathetically.

"I hope so," Alden replied. Suddenly his mood changed. He turned to Frank and Joe. "Now down to business. Your father tells me you two are going to work with him on the case," he said.

"That's right," Frank replied.

"Excellent! I'm sure you have some questions of your own you'll want to ask me. However, I must fly to Washington immediately after the competitions. How about all of us meeting in my office on Monday morning?"

The Hardys nodded.

Alden looked at his wrist watch. "It is time for me to get to my post. I'm the official timekeeper for the stock-car runs. Perhaps you would like to join me out on the track."

"Would we!" the boys answered excitedly.

As they started to walk off, Frank bent down and picked up a small packet which had fallen from his brother's pocket during the scuffle. It was Joe's detective kit. Each of the Hardys carried one. Among the items that had spilled out was a magnifying glass and a metal signalling mirror. He handed the kit to Joe.

Suddenly a voice crackled from the loudspeaker of the P.A. system.

"The first trial run will be made by car number twenty-two. The driver is Roger Alden!"

"What!" exploded Alden. "How did he get his hands on a car? I must stop him! Roger doesn't have enough experience for closed-circuit racing!"

·3·

Prime Suspect

ALDEN rushed towards the starting line with the Hardys close at his heels.

"Stop that car!" he shouted.

But it was too late. Roger roared off.

"Flag that car down!" Alden ordered one of the track officials.

"I'll try to signal him with my mirror when he comes along the straight," Joe said.

Frank and Joe ran alongside the track opposite to the direction Roger was heading. They watched him as he skidded dangerously on the far turn.

"Did you see that?" Frank yelled.

"Yes. He took that curve too fast."

The boys hurried down the straight. As Roger came round the second far turn, his car spun out of control and crashed through the fence on the sideline. A huge geyser of dust erupted from the spot.

Frank and Joe rushed to the scene of the accident. An ambulance sped by them with its siren screaming. They arrived just as two white-coated men were helping Roger move away from the damaged vehicle.

"Is he hurt?" Joe asked quickly.

"No," one of the men replied. "He's lucky. I think

he just had the wind knocked out of him. But we'll take him to the hospital for an examination, anyway."

Shortly Roger's father and Mr Hardy came running up.

"Are you all right?" Alden asked his son nervously.

"I—I guess so," Roger gasped, still trying to catch his breath. Then he glared at the Hardys and pointed an accusing finger at them. "You guys are the cause of this!" he screamed. "You reflected sunlight into my eyes with that mirror of yours!"

"You're crazy!" Joe retorted.

A rangy young man appeared and gazed at the wrecked car in disbelief. "My car!" he groaned. "It's almost totally demolished!"

"Are you the owner?" Alden queried.

"Yes, I am."

"How is it my son was driving your racer?"

"Roger offered me a hundred bucks if I would let him make the trial run," the young man explained. "Now all I have is a pile of junk."

"Serves you right," Alden snapped, "but I'll pay for the damage."

Roger was helped into the ambulance and taken to the hospital. Although his father was greatly upset over the incident, he did not request that the competitions be discontinued. Instead, Alden told the participants to carry on. At the signal, engines began roaring to life. The Hardys and Chet watched the day's activities and were thrilled by the performance of the skilful drivers.

After dropping Chet off at the Morton farm, the three detectives headed home. When they arrived, Mrs Hardy announced that supper was ready to be served. As they ate, the boys discussed the day's events.

Aunt Gertrude looked at them scornfully. "Racing of any kind is just dreadful! It should be outlawed!"

"When properly organized," Frank put in, "it's a fine sport."

"I call it utter nonsense!" Aunt Gertrude retorted. She hurried out of the room before her nephews could argue the point.

The next day the boys rose late. After eating a hearty breakfast and attending church services, they settled down to read the voluminous Sunday newspapers. Shortly the telephone rang. Frank scooped up the receiver. The caller was Iola Morton, Chet's sister.

"Chet won't be able to see you later," she sobbed. "He's had an accident!"

Frank and Joe leaped into their convertible and drove to the Morton farm. They arrived to find the entire family standing on the front porch of the house. Chet was seated on the steps, exclaiming that he was all right. His face was blackened with soot.

"I don't need a doctor!" the chubby youth insisted.

"What happened?" Frank asked worriedly.

Mr Morton, a good-looking, normally jolly man turned to the Hardys. "Chet was experimenting with a highly volatile fuel on the engine of that old car I keep in the barn. He was pouring some into the carburettor when it suddenly blew up."

"It seems the racing bug has bitten him," said Iola, a slim, pretty girl. She was a witty, light-hearted person and was a school chum of the Hardys. Iola was Joe's favourite date.

"I was afraid something like this would happen,"

Frank remarked. "However, I didn't expect it so soon."

Mrs Morton, an attractive, dark-haired woman, hurried to meet Dr Mills, a Bayport physician, as he drove up to the house. He examined Chet, then left after saying that fortunately the boy had not been injured.

"You'd better call off your experiments," Joe advised his friend.

"I'll make sure he does," Mr Morton said. "I'm getting rid of that old car right away."

"But you can't!" Chet protested. "I'm on the threshold of producing the Morton super-duty racing car!"

Frank and Joe helped to convince him that such experiments should be left to the experts. Chet was crestfallen for a moment, than his face suddenly brightened.

"I'll drop the race-car project in favour of another idea," he said. "A rocket-propelled bicycle!" The Hardys shook their heads in despair and returned home.

Monday morning found Mr Hardy and his sons in Keith Alden's office. The company president was seated comfortably behind his desk, ready to discuss the case with them.

Frank was the first to speak. "Dad says that you suspect someone is trying to steal your experimental motor. Why?"

"My motor," Alden replied, "uses a valve of a very unusual design. In fact, we're not equipped here at the plant to make one. However, I learned of a company on the West Coast that specializes in valve manufacturing. They said they could do the job, so I gave them the green light."

He went on to say that one day Mr Dillon, president of the valve company, had telephoned him excitedly. A stranger, who refused to identify himself, had appeared with the specifications of a valve exactly like the one to be used in Alden's experimental motor.

Keith Alden rubbed the back of his neck. "Beats me how the fellow got hold of my design."

"What's the name of the company, sir?" Joe asked.

"Exeter Valve. It's a small outfit and luckily for me very reputable. Mr Dillon told the guy he'd like to study the specifications further before agreeing to handle the job. The stranger refused and left."

"Did you get a description of him?" Frank asked.

"Yes," Alden replied. "He was tall, wore black-rimmed glasses, and had a beard and moustache that looked phony."

"Obviously a disguise," Mr Hardy commented.

"I'm certain it was by sheer accident that the stranger went to the same company I was dealing with," Alden declared. "And I'm also sure that his valve sketch was a direct copy of my own design."

"Leaping lizards!" Joe interjected. "Maybe the stranger has the plans to your whole motor!"

"We doubt that," Mr Hardy said.

Alden grinned. "Your father is referring to the precautions I have taken to prevent the plans from being stolen."

"What kind of precautions?" Frank asked.

Alden explained that there were only two sets of plans in existence. "One set, the original, is safely hidden. The other set is recorded on film slides."

"The work is divided among the technicians here," the man continued. "No one worker knows what the other is doing. Each receives his assignment in the form of a slide, which is placed in a burglarproof projector. He displays it on a small screen and uses it for his job."

"Sounds foolproof," Joe commented.

"That's what I thought," Alden said. "Yet somehow specifications for my motor must be leaking out of the plant."

"So far," Mr Hardy told his sons, "only half of the slides have ever been seen by anyone other than Mr Alden. That's why we doubt that the entire design has fallen into the wrong hands."

The boys asked Alden if he had the slightest reason to suspect any of his workers.

"No," he replied. "And just to be sure, I had them all double-checked."

"What about ex-employees?" Joe suggested. "Have you had any trouble in the past?"

Alden rubbed his chin dubiously. "Come to think of it, I did. But that was several months ago."

He stated that Vilno Sigor, an engineer and designer, had worked in his research department. The man had created a number of small, but clever inventions which were used by the company.

"Then one day Vilno came to my office and accused me of picking his brain," Alden said. "I told him that was what I was paying him for, and reminded him of the generous bonuses he received for his ideas. Vilno wanted more. He demanded a partnership in my firm.

When I refused, he became furious and left. I haven't seen him since."

"Too bad," Frank muttered. "He might have been our man."

"Now take his twin brother Barto," Alden remarked. "He's still employed in my research department as a sheet-metal worker. An excellent craftsman. His job is to fabricate the bodies of our experimental racing cars."

"A twin brother?" Frank exclaimed. "That's a lead. Barto could be in cahoots with Vilno!"

Alden grinned. "You'd be wasting your time investigating him. He's the direct opposite of Vilno in engineering knowledge and in temperament. Even if he got a look at the plans of my motor, he'd never be able to understand them."

Despite Alden's opinion of Barto, the boys were determined to list the sheet-metal worker as a prime suspect.

The young detectives asked about the two experimental cars that had met with accidents after their windshields had been mysteriously crazed. Alden told them that each of the vehicles was powered by a prototype of his motor.

"But whether the accidents were the result of sabotage, I can't say," he added.

Mr Hardy spoke up. "Right now let's tackle this case one step at a time," he advised his sons. "We have to assume that somewhere in this plant there's a clever crook. He's managing to steal specifications of the experimental motor. Our first job is to find out who he is. And we'll have to find him fast!"

·4·

Fingerprint Hunt

"So YOU want to work in my plant as undercover agents," Alden said, when told about the boys' plan. "I like the idea."

"Thanks," Frank replied. "When do we start?"

"Tomorrow, if that's all right with you fellows," Alden said. He glanced at his wrist watch. "I see it's nearly lunchtime. Let's have some food."

After a delicious meal in the company's cafeteria, Alden conducted the Hardys on a tour of the plant. The boys watched with interest as various machinists turned out parts for the experimental motor. Each of the men worked from a plan projected on a small screen.

The last item on the tour was a visit to the research department. There Alden introduced the boys and their father to Barto Sigor.

"I am pleased to meet you," Barto said in a quiet voice. He was a short, stocky man with bushy eyebrows and dark, wavy hair. His steel-grey eyes were fixed on the young detectives.

"These two lads will be working here in the plant for a while," Alden told him. "They're taking an automotive engineering course at school and would like to get a little practical experience."

"Ah," Barto responded. "So you want to learn the automobile business. That's good. Do not hesitate to call on me if you have any questions."

"We won't," Joe answered.

Later, while driving home to Bayport, Frank and Joe discussed the case with their father.

Then Joe said, "What's your opinion of Barto, Frank? He seems pleasant enough."

"I agree he's a weak suspect, but—"

"You have something on your mind, son," Mr Hardy guessed. "What is it?"

"Mr Alden said that Barto would not understand the motor specifications even if he got a look at the plans," Frank replied. "However, since Vilno and Barto are twins, it's possible that they could have switched identities."

"There's only one flaw in your theory," Mr Hardy said. "Vilno is not a sheet-metal worker. How could he perform his brother's job at the plant?"

"I didn't think about that," Frank admitted. "Still, I'd like to check it out."

"There's one way of settling the question," the older detective suggested. "Try to get Barto's fingerprints. But do it without his knowledge. We don't want Barto, or anyone else in the plant, to suspect you're working on a case."

The boys retired early that night. The next morning they started for the Alden plant immediately after breakfast. Mr Hardy, who had been supplied with a microfilm report of all the employees' records, remained at home to check the information against his files on criminals.

The boys spent the morning watching the skilled machinists perform their various tasks. Finally they positioned themselves so that they could peer into the research department to observe Barto. The young detectives noticed that he wore a pair of thin rubber gloves constantly. Joe made a casual remark about this to another mechanic.

"Barto always keeps those gloves on," the man said. "He uses certain acids in his work. Also, he says the gloves give him a better grip on his tools."

Eager to discuss the situation, the young detectives retreated to a secluded corner of the plant.

"Those gloves of Barto's make it impossible to get his fingerprints," Joe commented.

"He'll have to take them off some time," Frank pointed out. "Maybe when he has his lunch."

At noon most of the workers went to the cafeteria. Barto, however, did not leave the shop. Instead, he walked to a clothes rack in one corner of the room and pulled a sandwich, wrapped in wax paper, from the pocket of his jacket. He then sat down on a bench, removed his gloves, and unwrapped the sandwich. The boys watched from a distance.

"We might get a good print from that wax paper," Joe whispered.

"Right," his brother agreed. "Let's see what he does with it."

After Barto finished eating, he crumpled up the wax paper, put his gloves back on, and strolled out of the shop through an exit door. The young detectives rushed to a window and peered outside. There they spotted the suspect walking towards a flaming incinerator. The man tossed the wax paper into it and returned to the shop.

"Well, that's that," Joe muttered disappointedly.

"We can't waste too much time trying to get Barto's prints," Frank said. "Let's follow him when he quits work for the day."

A few minutes before five o'clock the boys hurried to the car park to pick up their car. Then they posted themselves outside the main gate. Workers began to spill out of the plant.

"There's Barto!" Joe said.

The boys watched their suspect walk to a street corner and wait. Soon a bus came along and Barto climbed aboard. The boys followed the vehicle. Eventually the trail led them to the centre of Clayton. The bus stopped and Barto got off.

"We'll park the car and follow him on foot," Frank declared.

They shadowed their suspect in the best detective fashion. Barto bought a newspaper. Then he stopped at a refreshment stand and ordered a glass of orange juice. When he had finished and walked off, Joe rushed to the stand to seize the glass. But before he could do so, the stand attendant swept up the tumbler and plunged it into a sink filled with soapy water.

"Out of luck again," Joe grumbled.

Finally Barto led the boys to a small, red-brick apartment house off the main street and entered the building. Frank and Joe waited a few minutes, then dashed into the lobby. They quickly checked the mailboxes and found that Barto lived in apartment 6B.

"Well, there's nothing more we can do today."

Frank sighed. "We may as well go home. Maybe we'll come up with an idea before tomorrow."

After supper the young detectives joined their father in his study.

"Sorry to hear you haven't had any luck with your investigation today," Mr Hardy said. "Neither have I. So far, none of Alden's employees show up in my criminal files."

"Did you check on Barto and his brother?" Frank queried.

"Yes, I have."

Mr Hardy said that according to their records, the twins had been born in a small Midwest community. When they were still very young, their father had moved the family to Switzerland, where he accepted a job as an engineer. It was there that Vilno attended a university, and Barto had learned the sheet-metal trade.

"The twins returned to the United States several years ago and started a business called Inventions, Incorporated," Mr Hardy continued. "They didn't do very well and finally closed the shop. After that, it was a matter of job-hopping until they joined the Alden company."

"Hm! Not much to go on there," Frank muttered. "However, I still want to follow through on the finger-print angle."

"Maybe we could get into Barto's apartment!" Joe suggested.

"We'd need a court order to do that," his brother said. "At present we haven't any reason for justifying such a move."

Frank thought for a moment, then suddenly sat bolt upright in his chair. "Wait a minute! I have an idea!" he exclaimed. "Barto has to grab the doorknob to enter his apartment. I can hide in the hallway and wait until he comes home, then simply lift his prints from the knob."

"Say! That might work!" Joe agreed.

"Go to it, boys. But be careful," Mr Hardy warned.

The hours dragged by slowly during the boys' second day at the plant. At lunch they reviewed their plan. Frank would leave an hour before stopping time and take the bus to Clayton. Joe would drive their car and shadow Barto as they had done the previous day.

A few minutes before four o'clock, Frank hurried from the plant and caught the bus to Clayton. Within half an hour he was climbing the stairs to the sixth floor where Barto's apartment was located. He found 6B, then stepped out through the exit door at the far end of the hallway. The young detective inched the door open so he could watch for his suspect.

"I hope Barto doesn't come home late tonight," he thought.

While Frank waited, an elderly woman in work clothes appeared with a vacuum cleaner and a small trash disposal cart. She unlocked Barto's door and went inside. Shortly she reappeared with a wastebasket and dumped its contents into the cart. Then she went back into the apartment. The whirling sound of a vacuum cleaner could be heard.

"I wonder what was in the wastebasket," Frank mused. "Maybe I'll find a clue."

He dashed to the cart and found several pieces of

crumpled paper. Frank jammed them into his pocket and returned to his hiding place.

Eventually the cleaning woman emerged from the room, locked the door, and disappeared down the hallway with her paraphernalia. Frank ran to the door and wiped it clean so that Barto's prints would be the only ones present.

Half an hour passed. Then, from his hiding place, Frank spotted Barto walking down the hallway. The stocky man unlocked his door, twisted the knob, and went inside. When the door closed behind him, Frank sprang into action.

He dusted the knob with a fine, grey powder. Next, he took a strip of sticky tape from a celluloid container and carefully pressed it on the knob. A split second later he lifted off the tape, placed it back in the container, then rushed down the stairs and out of the building. He saw Joe in their car about a block away.

"Whew!" Frank said, out of breath. "I was afraid Barto was going to open his door any second."

"Mission accomplished?" his brother asked half-jokingly.

Frank held up the celluloid container. "Here are his fingerprints. Let's take them to Chief Collig and have him check them right away."

The boys drove directly to Bayport Police Headquarters. Chief Collig told them that he would send the data to the FBI by teletype and call the Hardys as soon as he received a reply.

Arriving home, the boys had a leisurely supper, then went to their crime lab located above the garage. There they examined the crumpled pieces of paper

Frank had found in the disposal cart. All of them proved to be discarded advertising circulars, except one blank page.

"This looks like the backing sheet for a typewritten letter," Joe observed, as he carefully flattened it out on a table.

"Then there must be word impressions on it," his brother replied. "Let's put it under the ultra-violet light."

The boys treated the blank sheet with a chemical solution and placed it under a special lamp. Gradually, words began to show up clearly. The letter read:

6/2

Dear Eric:

Forgive me for taking so long to write you, but I've been so exhausted from work the last few days that I didn't feel I could write a coherent sentence. How I wish I had the stamina of two hard-working boys who have taken summer jobs at the plant. Any family would be proud to have sons like that.

As I already told you, my brother has left the Alden company. It came as a surprise to me because I did not detect anything in his behaviour to lead me to believe he was dissatisfied with his job. I hope he manages to survive his own idiosyncracies. His reasons for leaving were extremely unreasonable, and I hope he eventually sees the error of his ways.

Because of my brother, I feel a bit embarrassed about continuing to work here. I'm sure they're expecting me to leave also. I must admit I have been investigating other possible jobs, but now I realize it would be foolish of me to quit.

Hoping that luck will not continue to evade us, I am

Your friend,
Barto

The Hardys wondered to whom the letter had been sent, and if it might contain a coded message. After close examination, they concluded that the letter was quite ordinary. They kept it on file, nevertheless.

Later Chief Collig telephoned the boys. "I just got a reply on those prints you wanted checked," he announced. "They belong to a Barto Sigor."

The news was shattering. The Hardys no longer had a prime suspect!

·5·

A Close Call

THE next day and a half at the plant proved disappointing for the boys. Despite their meticulous investigation, they failed to come up with a suspect.

"I'm ready to tackle this case from another angle," Frank said. "We may as well give up our undercover work here at the plant. Nothing more we can do."

"What do you have in mind?" Joe asked.

"Looking into the accidents involving Alden's experimental racing cars."

"Do you think there's some connection between the accidents and the stealing of the motor specifications?"

Frank shrugged. "I don't know. Each of the cars was equipped with a prototype model of the motor. Yet why would anyone risk destroying the cars if that's what they were after?"

"Let's have a talk with Alden," Joe suggested.

In a little while the boys were seated in the president's office.

"So you want to investigate the accidents," Alden said. "That's okay with me."

"We'd like to have a talk with the drivers," Frank replied.

38

"You'll find them in the garage opposite the research department," Alden told the boys. "They're getting another of my cars ready for a road race competition that's coming up. Their names are Jim Markus and Speed Johnston."

Frank and Joe made their way towards a large, metal-covered building. Inside, a crew of mechanics was busy working on a bright red experimental racing car. Two wiry young men, in their mid-twenties, were watching the proceedings. They turned when the boys called out the names of the drivers.

"I'm Jim Markus," one of them said.

"And my name's Speed Johnston," announced the other, extending his hand in greeting. "What can we do for you?"

Frank and Joe questioned the drivers about their accidents. They told the Hardys that Alden had entered the experimental vehicles in the competitions in order to match their performance against other makes of cars. The explanation of the accidents were the same as Alden had given, except for a couple of interesting facts. First, each of the drivers had experienced a crazing of the windshield immediately after turning a sharp bend in the road. Shortly before it happened, each of them recalled seeing a sign marked DANGER.

"Would you show us on a map where the accidents took place?" Frank asked.

"Sure thing," Johnston replied.

He took out a road map and spread it on the floor. "Mine happened here," he said, jabbing a finger at the spot along a winding red line.

Markus stooped beside his companion. "And my accident took place right here," he added, marking the location with a pencil.

The boys thanked the drivers for their help, then left, taking the map with them.

"The road isn't far from here," Frank commented. "Joe, let's drive there and take a look around."

Half an hour later the Hardys were guiding their convertible along a narrow, winding road. They arrived at the sharply curved segment indicated by Johnston and stopped.

"This is the spot," Frank remarked. "But I don't see a sign marked DANGER."

The boys got out and walked along the shoulder of the road.

"Look!" Joe exclaimed, pointing down at the ground. "There's a little mound of dirt. Someone has filled in a small hole."

"You're right," his brother agreed. "That's where the sign must have been. But why was it taken away?"

Puzzled, the boys returned to their car and drove on to the spot where Markus had said he had his accident. It proved to be another sharply curved segment on the road. The Hardys again examined the shoulder and found a similar mound of dirt.

"Strange," Frank muttered. "I think we're on to something. The only problem is—what?"

It was getting late, so the boys decided to drive home. When they arrived, Mrs Hardy rushed out of the house to meet them.

"Something has happened to your Aunt Gertrude!" she cried out.

"Where is she?" Frank asked.

"In the living room!"

The boys quickly followed their mother inside. There they found Aunt Gertrude slumped in a chair. Mrs Hardy had placed a wet towel on her forehead.

"What's wrong, Aunt Gertrude?" Frank asked.

Miss Hardy suddenly came to life. "The telegram I just received!" she moaned. "What a dreadful inheritance! Read it!"

The boys looked down and saw the telegram on the floor beside her chair. Joe picked it up and they read the message. Both tried hard not to laugh.

"So that's what this is all about," Frank said finally. "You've inherited a stable of race horses."

"A stable of retired race horses, you mean!" she exclaimed. "They're the worst kind. They've already fleeced the public!"

Mrs Hardy smiled. "I think it's wonderful," she commented. "You might get to like horses. They seem to grow on you in time."

"Laura! How can you say such a thing!" Aunt Gertrude rebuked her. She slumped back in her chair. "And to think that this was wished on me by an old friend I forgot even existed. She apparently has no heirs."

"Where is the stable located?" Joe queried.

"In Baltimore," his aunt replied. "Even that is too close for me."

"What do you plan to do with it?" Frank asked.

"Sell the place!" Aunt Gertrude shot back. "And the quicker the better!"

"Now calm down," Mrs Hardy urged. "Tomorrow we'll telephone the attorney handling the estate and see what this is all about."

Aunt Gertrude remained silent all through supper. Finally a teasing cry of "Giddap!" from Joe sent her storming out of the room.

The next morning the boys went straight to Alden's office. They told him about the signs the drivers had mentioned and of their own investigation.

"Sounds mysterious," Alden remarked. "But what harm could a sign do?"

"I can't answer that at the moment," Frank admitted. "But I've a hunch it has something to do with the accidents."

Alden eyed the boys with interest. "How do you plan to follow up your hunch?"

"The last time we talked," Frank recalled, "you said that another of your experimental cars was being got ready for a road race."

"That's right. In fact, the race is scheduled for tomorrow."

"Where is it to take place?" Frank asked.

"On a road not far from the one where the accidents happened. Why?" Alden asked.

"If you'll point out the road for us on a map," Frank explained, "Joe and I will travel the route shortly before the race starts. Maybe we'll spot one of those signs. At least it's worth a try."

Alden pulled a map from his desk drawer and indicated the road to be used for the competition. Then the boys returned home and discussed the plan with their father.

"You might be on to something," Mr Hardy said. "I'll drive the route with you."

"Thanks, Dad," Frank replied. "But we weren't going to use the car."

"You're not planning to walk all the way?" the detective asked with a look of astonishment. "The race will be over a course of several miles."

"We discussed it on the way home, Dad," Joe put in. "We plan to use our old bicycles. They're still stored in the garage."

Mr Hardy leaned back in his chair and grinned. "I get it. Bicycles are noiseless. And if there is anything behind this sign theory of yours, you won't scare off whoever's setting them up."

"Exactly," Frank replied.

Before retiring for the night, the boys went to the garage and inspected their bicycles.

"The tyres have to be inflated, and a few drops of oil are needed here and there," Joe observed. "Otherwise, they're in good shape."

It took only a few minutes to do the job, then they rode their bicycles once around the block for a quick test run.

"Let's load the bikes in our car," Frank suggested, "so we'll be all set to go first thing in the morning."

Frank and Joe got an early start. Mr Hardy accompanied them to the starting line. There were about twenty stock cars lined up for the race. Each was painted in a different colour scheme. Drivers and mechanics were milling around, waiting for the contest to begin. Alden was there and greeted the Hardys.

"How much time do we have before the race gets under way?" Frank asked him.

"About thirty minutes. My car will be the first one off. Johnston is the driver."

"Then we'd better get going right away," Frank declared.

"Be careful," Mr Hardy urged.

The young detectives lifted their bicycles from the boot, then pedalled down the road.

After they had covered most of the route, Joe sighed. "I'd forgotten how slow bicycling can be."

"Keep going," his brother said. "The race will be starting any second now, and it won't take the cars long to travel this far. We should cover as much of the route as we can before they do."

As the boys continued, they noticed that the road was becoming treacherous for racing. It was flanked on one side by a rocky wall, and on the other by a sloping embankment with a drop of nearly a hundred feet.

Eventually Frank and Joe came to a sharp bend in the road. As they rounded it, Frank suddenly locked his brakes. Joe did the same. Just ahead was a large sign marked DANGER!

"Leaping lizards!" Joe declared in a hushed voice.

"That sign is exactly like the ones Johnston and Markus described to us," Frank observed. "Let's take a look at it."

"Maybe we're being watched."

"That's a chance we'll have to take."

The boys laid their bicycles on the embankment and began walking towards the sign. When they reached it, they stopped and gazed at its face.

"What do you make of it?" Joe queried.

"Seems quite ordinary, except for one thing," Frank answered. "It's much thicker than most signs."

At that instant the young detectives heard a faint, whirring noise.

"What's that?" Joe said.

Frank listened. "I'd say it's a generator of some kind," he concluded.

"It's coming from a spot a little farther down the road."

The boys began to inch their way towards the source of the sound. Suddenly the roar of a motor became distinct. Each second it grew louder.

"The first of the racing cars is coming!" Joe gasped.

The Hardys turned just in time to see Alden's entry tearing around the sharp curve in the road. Suddenly it began to swerve out of control. The vehicle bounced into the air and hurtled directly towards the boys!

· 6 ·

Final Warning

THE racing car plunged towards Frank and Joe like some horrible monster eager to crush its prey. In a desperate move the boys leaped down the embankment and went tumbling head over heels to the bottom. They lay stunned. The next thing they knew, Mr Hardy and Alden were leaning over them.

"Are you all right?" their father asked anxiously.

"I'm—I'm okay," Frank assured him.

"Me too," Joe added, rubbing his head gingerly.

"One of the other drivers saw that there had been an accident and reported it," Alden said. "We got here just as fast as we could."

Frank sprang to his feet. "Your driver, Johnston! How is he?"

"Fine, except for a few bruises," Alden replied. He grinned. "I build very strong cars. My drivers are well protected."

The boys told the two men what they had seen.

"And you say there was a signpost marked DANGER?" Mr Hardy asked curiously. "Where?"

Frank pointed towards the top of the embankment. "The one right—" His words trailed off.

"Why—it's gone!" Joe exclaimed.

The boys led the way up the embankment. Then

they slowly walked along the shoulder of the road. In a minute they discovered a small hole that had been hastily filled in.

"Here's the place," Frank said. "This is where we saw the sign."

"I'd call it a sinister signpost," Mr Hardy remarked, rubbing his chin dubiously. "It's here one minute, and gone the next. Obviously someone has carried it off."

Joe casually thrust his hands into the pockets of his jacket. A moment later his face showed surprise and he pulled a piece of paper from one of his pockets. On it was a printed message:

THIS IS A FINAL WARNING!
HANDS OFF THE ALDEN CASE!

"This must have been put in my pocket while we were lying at the bottom of the embankment," Joe said.

"We can be sure of one thing," Frank added. "Whoever's after Mr Alden's experimental motor is also responsible for the accidents."

A car roared up and screeched to a halt. Its driver, one of Alden's racing car mechanics, leaped out.

"Mr Alden!" he shouted excitedly. "We just received a call from one of your watchmen at the plant. The research department is on fire!"

"We'll drive you there," Mr Hardy offered. "There might be a connection with the accident here."

He and his sons hopped into the boys' convertible with Alden. By the time they arrived at the plant, the flames were completely extinguished. Firemen began to rummage through a charred area that once was Alden's research shop.

"This is a terrible blow to my experimental project," he muttered.

The Hardys expressed their regret, then went to talk with the fire chief.

"I can't say what caused the fire," the chief told them. "We'll have to conduct an investigation first."

"Approximately when did it start?" Frank asked.

"We got the alarm about an hour ago."

"I'd appreciate knowing the results of your investigation," Mr Hardy said as he presented his credentials to the fire chief.

The man recognized the name immediately. "It sure is a pleasure to meet you, sir. And these two boys must be your sons, Frank and Joe. My name's Fred Evans." There was an exchange of handshakes. "You can count on me," the fire chief continued. "I'll let you know if we uncover anything."

The Hardys thanked him, then rejoined Alden, who was picking his way through the rubble of his burned shop.

"There's nothing left to salvage," he said dejectedly. "However, I'll set up a temporary research shop in one of the other buildings."

The Hardys expressed their regrets at Alden's loss and returned home. Aunt Gertrude was still greatly upset over her inheritance of a stable filled with retired race horses.

"Fenton!" she exclaimed. "You promised to call the attorney who's handling the estate, and you never did. Please do it right away. I can't rest thinking about that awful place."

Mr Hardy went to telephone, while the boys had a

snack of sandwiches and milk in the kitchen. A few minutes later their father hurried into the room.

"I still have the attorney on the line," Mr Hardy said. "He'd like us to take a look at the stables. However, I have too much work to clean up here, and I'm sure your aunt won't go. So why don't you two boys hop down to Maryland?"

"Sure thing, Dad," Frank replied.

Mr Hardy completed his call, then gave Frank and Joe their instructions.

"You can catch an early train to Baltimore in the morning," the detective explained. "The attorney will meet you at the station there. He'll be waiting in front of the information desk. His name is Steve Benson."

Frank and Joe left Bayport aboard the seven o'clock train. It was nearly noon when they arrived in Baltimore. The boys went directly to the information desk and noticed a tall, even-featured man standing nearby. He appeared to be in his late fifties, and was impeccably dressed.

"Mr Benson?" Frank queried.

"Yes," the man answered. "And you must be the Hardys. I've heard a lot about you and your father." He extended his hand in greeting. "My car is just outside. The stable isn't far from here."

The boys enjoyed the drive through the lush, green countryside. During the journey, the attorney discussed Aunt Gertrude's situation.

"Your father says that she wants to sell the stable as soon as possible," Benson remarked. "We shouldn't have any trouble doing that. In fact, Norman Fowler, the temporary manager out there, would like to buy the place. Unfortunately he doesn't have the money right now."

Nearly an hour passed before Benson guided his car through an arched gateway. Spread across the arch, in gold letters, was the name:

SOUTHERN PINES STABLES

"All told, there are about twenty acres here," the attorney announced. "It's not very big, but it's adequate for the purpose."

Ahead, the boys saw a small house and two other wooden structures. All were painted white and appeared to be in excellent condition. The largest of the buildings contained the stalls for the horses. To the left was a large grassy area surrounded by a wooden fence. About a dozen fine-looking horses were lazily grazing there.

Benson brought the car to a stop near the house and got out. The young detectives followed. Standing on the porch was a bulky, deeply tanned man whom the attorney introduced to the boys as Norman Fowler.

"The Hardys have come to take a look round," Benson told him.

"Glad to be of service," Fowler said cordially. "As you probably know, all the horses here have seen the last of their racing days. The owners want to provide a comfortable retirement for them. That's our job."

The manager invited his guests into the house to lunch, then took them on a tour of the stables. As the day drew to a close, Fowler suggested that the boys remain overnight and return to Bayport in the morning.

"All my stable hands are away for the evening at a

local affair," he said, "and the bunkhouse is empty. You can sleep there."

Benson announced that he had to leave, but promised to return in the morning to drive the Hardys to the railroad station. After a quick supper prepared by Fowler, Frank and Joe went to the bunkhouse. At ten o'clock they retired for the night. Little more than an hour had passed when the boys were awakened by the muffled sound of men talking.

"That's odd," Frank whispered. "I thought all of Fowler's stable hands were away for the evening."

The boys dressed and crept out of the bunkhouse towards the source of the voices.

"We want fifty per cent of the take," they heard one man say.

Joe accidentally stepped on a twig, which snapped with a cracking noise. The boys froze in their tracks and listened. There was only silence.

"Let's move ahead and try to get a glimpse of the men," Frank hissed.

The young detectives cautiously edged their way through the darkness. They saw no one. Then suddenly a voice boomed out from behind them.

"Stay where you are!"

The boys turned to find themselves peering into the muzzle of a rifle.

"Who are you?" Joe demanded.

The armed man directed the beam of a flashlight into the faces of the Hardys.

"Oh, it's you boys," he said. "I thought you were asleep." The man flicked the beam of light on to his own face.

"Mr Fowler!" Frank exclaimed.

"We heard some men talking out here," Joe explained, "and came to investigate."

"Did you see them?" the manager questioned.

"No," Frank replied. "We never got close enough."

"Well, I heard them too," Fowler said. "But I'm sure they were workers from the farm just across the way. They often use our area as a short cut when they walk back from town." He then said good night and went into the house.

Frank and Joe rose early the next morning. They had just finished breakfast when Benson arrived to take them to the railroad station. The boys thanked Fowler for his hospitality, then hurried off to the train. During the drive, the attorney explained some of the legal points involved in their aunt's intended sale, and handed them some documents that she was to examine.

When they arrived in Bayport, the boys wasted no time in telling Aunt Gertrude and their parents what they had seen.

"It's too bad you want to sell the stable," Joe said. "The place is beautiful."

"Say no more!" their aunt retorted. "Just give me the documents the lawyer wants me to read, so that I can get it over with!"

"Once your aunt makes up her mind," Mr Hardy commented, "there's no changing it."

The following morning Alden telephoned Mr Hardy. "Come to the Clayton Police Station right away," he requested. "There's a thief down here who's been stealing information on my experimental motor!"

·7·

The Elusive Stranger

MR HARDY and the boys drove to Clayton immediately. Alden met them at the police station.

"Where is the suspect?" Mr Hardy asked him.

"Detective Lieutenant Swaze is questioning him in the interrogation room," Alden answered. "He said we were to join him the minute you arrived."

Inside, a thin, untidily dressed man was seated in a chair. Lieutenant Swaze, lanky and middle-aged, was pacing the floor in front of him. Alden introduced the detective to the Hardys.

"This man is charged with burglary," Swaze announced. "He was caught rifling Mr Alden's office safe by one of the watchmen at the plant."

"When the police searched him," Alden interrupted, "they found several hollow-core impeller blades for my experimental motor in his pocket. I always keep a supply of them in the safe until an engine is ready for assembly."

Mr Hardy turned to the suspect. "Whom are you working for?" he demanded.

"I ain't workin' for nobody!" the prisoner shouted. "And I don't know nothin' about any experimental motor!"

"Then why did you take the impeller blades?" Frank asked quickly.

"Them things were made out o' shiny metal," the man replied nervously. "I thought it might be silver and I could get some money for 'em."

The interrogation continued for another two hours. The prisoner stuck to his story. Finally the boys and their father left the room with Alden.

"I'm convinced the suspect is telling the truth," Mr Hardy concluded. "He's obviously just a small-time crook who would steal anything."

"Then you don't think he's part of a gang trying to get the plans for my motor?" Alden queried.

"At this point, no," the detective said. "But let's see what the police come up with when they check his record."

Alden glanced at his watch and announced that he would have to return to the plant. The Hardys walked to their car and started back to Bayport, disappointed that nothing had come of their trip.

While driving through the centre of Clayton, Joe suddenly pointed towards two men standing at a street corner. "Look!" he exclaimed. "There's Barto talking to someone!"

"I wonder why he's not at work," Frank remarked.

"Maybe he has the day off," Joe answered.

The boys noticed that Barto's companion had the collar of his jacket turned up high, and his hat pulled low over his eyes.

"That guy he's with sure looks suspicious," Joe commented.

Frank stopped the car at the next corner. "I'll walk

past Barto and try to get a glimpse of the other man's face," he said. "The sidewalk is crowded with pedestrians. Chances are he won't spot me."

Frank made his way towards the two men. When he was within a few feet of them, Barto suddenly gave his companion a hard shove. The man turned and ran down the street. Frank, figuring this was strange, raced off in pursuit.

"Did you see that?" Joe said to his father.

"Yes! Come on! Frank might need our help!"

They leaped out of the car and joined in the chase. Mr Hardy stopped long enough to fire a question at Barto.

"Who was that man you were talking to?"

Barto appeared surprised. "I—I don't know," he stammered. "He was looking for a handout. When I refused, he insulted me and I gave him a shove."

Mr Hardy hurried on and found his sons standing at the entrance of an office building.

"He ran in here," Frank told his father.

"Let's go after him!" Joe urged.

"I'll stay outside," Mr Hardy said. "In case he gives you the slip, I'll go after him."

The boys ran into the building and discovered that the elevator was out of order. They bounded up the stairs. High above them, the two sleuths heard heavy footsteps.

"He must be heading for the roof!" Joe whispered.

Continuing the chase, the boys soon reached the roof. Their quarry was not in sight, but they heard what sounded like a metal door being slammed shut.

"It came from over there!" Joe said, pointing to the roof of an adjacent building.

The boys leaped across the narrow gap separating the two structures, and found a door leading inside. Pulling it open, Frank and Joe rushed down the stairs to the ground floor. Their father met them as they dashed outside.

"Your man came running out of this building," Mr Hardy said. "I was too far away to stop him. By the time I realized what had happened, he disappeared in the crowd."

"Too bad," said Frank.

As the Hardys drove home, the detective told his sons what Barto had said.

"Do you believe him?" Frank asked.

"We have no choice but to take his word for it," Mr Hardy replied. "Yet Barto doesn't strike me as the type that goes shoving people around."

"And why would a man just asking for a handout run off like a fugitive?" Joe interjected.

"There's something fishy about this," Frank added.

The Hardys had just finished supper when the telephone rang. Frank answered.

"This is Mr Alden," the caller said. "I have one more completed racing car fitted with my experimental engine. Luckily it was in the garage when the research shop burned down. I plan to give it a test run to-morrow."

"Another competition?" Frank asked.

"No, this will be a private test. I have permission from the highway department to use a straight stretch of road near the plant. I'd like you boys and your father to be present. I don't expect any trouble, but it pays to be safe."

"Wouldn't it be better to use the drag strip at your track?" Frank suggested. "You'd be less likely to find intruders there."

"The strip is too short for my purpose," Alden explained. "Shall we say ten o'clock tomorrow morning?"

"We'll be there," Frank assured him.

The next day the boys and their father drove to the test site. Alden's experimental racing car was unpainted, and its highly polished metal surface gleamed in the sun. Mechanics were giving the vehicle a final inspection.

"We'll be ready to start in about twenty minutes," Alden told the boys. "I intend to drive the first couple of runs myself. They will be acceleration tests."

He said that the car was a two-seater designed to carry a mechanic in addition to the driver.

"Since I won't be taking a mechanic with me," Alden said, "how would one of you boys like to go along?"

He suggested that the boys draw straws to decide which one would accompany him. They did, and Frank won.

"That's settled," Alden remarked, then added, "Joe, would you mind helping us with the tests?"

"How?"

"Normally, there's not any traffic using this road," Alden replied. "But we can't be sure. So I'd like to post a man with a walkie-talkie at the far end of the stretch to warn me if anything comes along. I have a radio receiver in the car for that purpose."

"I'm your man," Joe assured him.

He could not help but feel a bit envious of his brother as he watched Frank climb into the sleek car with Alden. Mr Hardy drove Joe to his post a couple of miles down the road, which at that point was flanked by heavy woods.

As the detective drove off, Joe heard a voice crackle from the speaker of his walkie-talkie. "All clear ahead?"

"All clear!"

Minutes later, Joe could detect the sound of Alden's car approaching. Then he spotted it far down the road. It was a shining speck of silver that grew larger and larger each second.

As Joe watched, he was startled to see a battered car emerge from the woods.

"Stop!" Joe cried frantically. "Mr Alden, stop!"

·8·

Stolen!

THE dilapidated car turned on to the road, picked up speed, and headed directly for Alden's car. Joe raced after it, calling out into the walkie-talkie.

His pleas went unheeded. Joe was horror-stricken at the small gap between the two vehicles. A head-on collision seemed inevitable.

"Frank! Mr Alden!" Joe screamed. "Watch out!"

Suddenly the mystery car swerved out of control. It went hurtling off the road and tumbled over into a ditch. A split second later the vehicle was a mass of flames.

Alden brought his racer to a screeching halt. He and Frank leaped out and followed Joe towards the disabled vehicle. They managed to get close enough to pull open one of its doors. The three were amazed to find that there was no one inside.

"Get back!" Alden shouted. "The tank may explode any second."

His warning came just in time. As Alden and the boys got clear, there was an explosion. A large ball of orange flame rose above the burning car. It was quickly transformed into a thick cloud of black smoke.

Minutes later a pickup truck arrived on the scene,

carrying a crew of Alden's mechanics. Mr Hardy was with them. The men scrambled out with fire extinguishers, and directed streams of chemical foam at the burning car. Soon the flames and smoke disappeared.

"You gave us a bad scare," Mr Hardy said, turning to Frank and Alden. "We saw the smoke and came running. We thought you'd had an accident with the car."

"They almost did," Joe said shakily. He told his father what had happened.

When the car cooled sufficiently to be touched, the Hardys examined it. The heat had turned the vehicle into a charred mass of twisted metal.

Frank, looking underneath, made a startling discovery. To the underside was attached the remains of an elaborate radio-controlled system. Wires ran from it to the throttle and steering mechanism.

"So that's how the car was operated with no driver!" Joe exclaimed. "But why did it go haywire all of a sudden?"

Frank had an answer. "When Joe used the walkie-talkie to warn us, the signal must have interfered with the radio frequency used to guide the car."

Mr Hardy nodded. "Whoever operated the transmitter would have needed a clear view of the road, and at a point not too far away from this spot."

Frank looked towards a high hill, the top of which loomed above the treetops. "There's a perfect spot," he said, pointing to it.

The boys lost no time in climbing to the summit to investigate. The area was covered with thick brush and grass.

"These bushes would provide good cover for anyone watching the road," Frank stated.

"Look! Over here!" Joe cried out. "Some of the grass has been trampled flat. I'd say it was done recently by two or three men."

Frank examined the spot. "This is where the transmitter was set up," he concluded. "From here you get a perfect view of the road."

A further search revealed no other clues. The boys rejoined their father and Alden. Mr Hardy stated that he had given the mystery car a thorough going-over, but found nothing that would permit them to trace its owner.

"The vehicle wasn't carrying licence plates, and the serial numbers on the engine and chassis had been removed," he continued. "Also, the fact that it was burned to a crisp doesn't help either."

Alden decided to carry on with the tests. When he had finished, the Hardys offered to drive him to his office.

As they started off, Alden rested back in the seat. "After all the excitement we've been having lately, I need a little diversion," he said. "I think I'll spend Saturday giving my race horse a workout."

"Race horse?" Joe queried.

"Yes," Alden answered. "I'm interested in racing of all kinds. I bought the horse several months ago. Great animal! I keep him in a rented stable near the plant."

"Our aunt would tell you off quickly if she knew this," Frank remarked laughingly. He then told Alden about Gertrude Hardy's recent inheritance.

"A stable for retired race horses? Sounds like a great

idea," Alden said. "I'll keep it in mind. Perhaps some day I'll send my horse down there."

"Not if Aunt Gertrude has anything to say about it," Joe muttered with a grin. "Anyway, she will have sold her stable by that time."

Alden asked the Hardys if they would like to see his horse. The boys' father had to decline because of a business appointment, but Frank and Joe eagerly accepted the invitation.

"And would you mind if we bring our friend Chet?" Frank asked.

"Please do," Alden replied. "Drop by any time. I'll be at the stable most of the day."

Chet was not able to go until the afternoon because of Saturday chores to do. The Hardys picked him up at the Morton farm.

"A real race horse, eh?" Chet said with a grin. He pulled three apples from his pockets and offered one to each of his friends. "What I wouldn't give to own one!"

When they arrived at the stables, Alden was leading a beautiful, haltered thoroughbred around the paddock. His owner spotted the boys and led the animal towards them.

"How do you like him?" he called out. "His name is Topnotch."

"Nice piece of horseflesh," Chet commented, trying to act like a seasoned equestrian.

The horse was completely chestnut in colour, except for small white areas above its two front hoofs. The boys watched in admiration as Alden removed the halter and permitted Topnotch to trot freely round the paddock.

As Joe glanced towards a row of stalls nearby, he noticed a sandy-haired young man pitching hay into one of them.

"Mr Alden, isn't that your son Roger over there?" Joe asked.

"Yes," Alden replied in a determined voice. "I arranged to get him a job here so that he could help pay for the racing car he damaged. It's about time he developed a sense of responsibility. I'd have given him something to do at the plant, but he can't get along with the other workers."

Chet followed the Hardys to the stall.

"Hello, Roger," Frank said in a friendly voice.

The young man looked surprised. Then his eyes narrowed as he glared at the boys.

"Oh, it's you guys again!" he snapped. "You keep popping up like bad dreams."

"So you're still carrying a chip on your shoulder," Joe retorted.

"You bet I am," Roger shot back angrily. "I've got to work in this lousy place to pay for that stock-race car I had an accident in. You Hardys were the cause of it all!"

Frank kept his temper, but said, "Don't tell us you're sticking to that fairy tale of yours. You know we didn't reflect sunlight into your eyes while you were driving."

"It's my word against yours," Roger snarled. "But what chance do I stand? Because you're the Hardy boys you think you can get away with anything."

Joe's face flushed with anger. However, he managed to exercise self-control. "It's useless trying to talk sense into Roger," he said. "We'd better go."

As they walked away, Chet remarked, "That fellow is about as friendly as an enraged cobra."

Roger, who overheard the comment, gave Chet a black look. He picked up a large mass of hay with his pitchfork and flung it on top of the chubby youth.

Chet scrambled from underneath the pile. He quickly brushed strands of hay from his eyes, ears, and hair. Then, angry, he grabbed a feed bag nearby and pulled it over Roger's head, down to his elbows. The imprisoned boy stumbled around the stall in a frenzy.

"I'll get you for this!" Roger yelled after his tormentor, when he finally pulled the bag free.

The Hardys and their chum strolled back to the paddock. Mr Alden had been too preoccupied with Topnotch to notice what had happened.

"Let's not say anything to him about Roger," Frank suggested.

The boys spent the rest of the afternoon watching Alden exercise his horse, or taking turns riding the mount themselves.

"He's super," Chet remarked. "Sure beats our farm horses."

At sundown the boys thanked the owner and left.

Frank and Joe spent a relaxing Sunday at home and retired early. The family had been asleep only a short time when the telephone rang. Frank got up and rushed to answer it. His father had already picked up the extension by his bed.

"This is Alden," an excited voice was saying. "Sorry to disturb you. But something terrible has happened and I need your help. I'm at the stable. Topnotch has been stolen!"

·9·

Demand for Ransom

FRANK wakened his brother to tell him about Top-notch. The boys and their father dressed quickly, rushed to their car, and headed for the stable.

"This sounds to me like some of Roger's work," Joe suggested.

"Possibly," Frank agreed. "He's pretty mad at his father. Roger could have done it for spite. But stealing a horse is not easy. He'd need help."

"My advice is to wait until we get the facts before coming to any conclusions," Mr Hardy interjected. "I realize Roger would never win a popularity contest. Yet it's hard to believe he'd be mean enough to do a thing like this."

They arrived at the stable to find Alden still greatly distraught over the theft of his horse.

"The police were here to investigate," he told the Hardys. "They left a few minutes ago."

"What did they come up with?" Joe asked.

"Nothing," Alden replied disappointedly. "The thieves were careful not to leave a shred of evidence behind. Even the foot and hoofprints leading from Topnotch's stall were swept away."

"But they must have used some kind of vehicle to carry the horse off," Frank said. "Did the police find any tyre tracks in the area?"

Alden nodded and asked the Hardys to follow him. After walking a short distance, he directed the beam of his flashlight towards the ground and pointed to a set of deep, parallel ruts pressed into the soft earth.

"They must have been made by a truck or a horse van," Joe said.

Mr Hardy stooped down and examined the ruts carefully. "Obviously the thieves covered the wheels with canvas or other heavy material," he concluded. "There aren't any tread marks. Too bad."

"Were there any witnesses to the crime?" Frank queried.

"Only one of the grooms," Alden answered. "But he can't help us. He lives in a room above the stable. When he heard a strange noise in one of the stalls, he came down to investigate and was struck from behind. The police took him to the hospital."

"Has the groom been able to tell when the theft took place?" Mr Hardy questioned.

"Yes. He regained consciousness. The theft was about five hours ago. The groom had been tied and gagged. It took him over four hours to work himself free after he regained consciousness."

Joe let out a whistle. "Five hours!" he exclaimed. "The truck could be hundreds of miles away by now."

The Hardys did not want to upset Alden any further by asking him about Roger's whereabouts that evening. Instead, they discussed the case from another angle.

"We don't know if this was an inside job or not,"

Mr Hardy remarked. "But we can be reasonably sure what the motive is. Ransom!"

"In that case, the thieves will try to contact me," Alden said. "If they do it by telephone, they'll call my office, since I have an unlisted number at home."

"I suggest we go there right away and wait," Frank put in. "The horse thieves may start to call early."

Alden accompanied the Hardys in their car. During the drive, Mr Hardy outlined a basic plan.

"If you should receive a call demanding ransom," he advised the horse's owner, "stall him off. Tell him you want proof that they actually have Topnotch. That'll give us more time to hunt for a lead."

Arriving at the plant, Alden led the way to his office. There he and his companions each selected a comfortable chair and settled down to wait.

"Have you a private line here in addition to your regular company phone?" Mr Hardy asked the executive.

"Yes, I do," Alden replied, pointing to one of two phones on his desk.

"Good," the elder detective said. "I'll use it to have the call traced if the thieves should contact you."

The night dragged on slowly. The boys were restless and found it difficult to sleep. When morning finally came, Alden arranged to have breakfast served in his office.

It was a little after nine when there was a short buzz on the company phone. Alden scooped it up, listened for a moment, then covered the mouthpiece with his hand.

"It's my secretary in the outer office," he informed

the Hardys. "She says a man wants to speak to me. He refuses to identify himself."

"This might be the call we're waiting for!" Joe exclaimed softly.

Mr Hardy rushed to the private phone. "I'll get to work on having the number traced," he announced quickly. Seconds later, he signalled Alden to proceed.

"Okay, put him on," Alden ordered his secretary.

The boys fixed their eyes on the executive and waited anxiously.

Alden suddenly sat bolt upright in his chair. "You want fifty thousand dollars' ransom to return Topnotch?" he shouted into the phone. "You're out of your mind! I'd want absolute proof before I handed out that kind of money!"

A few seconds later the executive put the phone down. "He hung up," Alden announced.

Mr Hardy frowned. "Too bad. There wasn't enough time to trace the call. Obviously we're not dealing with amateurs."

"What did he say when you asked for proof that they had Topnotch?" Frank put in.

"He said he'd think about it and let me know later," Alden replied.

Mr Hardy stretched out his arms and yawned. "You boys must be as exhausted as we are," he said. "Why don't you go home and get some rest? I'll stay here. You'll hear from me immediately if anything comes up."

His sons readily agreed. But it was not rest that interested them. Their father's suggestion offered an

"You want fifty thousand dollars' ransom?" Alden
shouted

excellent opportunity for them to question Roger without Alden's knowledge.

"Let's go back to the stable and see if he's working today," Frank said, as they drove off in their convertible.

When the Hardys arrived, Roger was busy painting a section of the fence that surrounded the paddock.

"We'd like to ask you a few questions," Frank called out.

Roger quickly glanced at his visitors without interrupting his work. "It's you guys again!" he snapped. "Haven't you got a home? Get lost! I don't have time to answer any of your stupid questions."

"Come off it!" Joe shot back angrily. "You must know your father's horse was stolen last night. That's what we want to ask you about."

There was a momentary pause. Roger nervously fingered his paintbrush and kept his face turned away from the Hardys. "Yes, I heard about it," he muttered defiantly. "But you've come to the wrong guy for information. And even if I did know something about it, I wouldn't tell you."

"Where were you last night?" Frank demanded.

"Why don't you try looking into a crystal ball to find out?" the young man retorted.

"Cut the comedy!" Joe exclaimed. "This is serious. A theft has been committed, and there's no reason why you shouldn't be among the suspects."

"Okay! If you have to know, I was working on my dragster all evening," Roger snapped.

"Where?" Frank questioned.

"At home!"

"Can you prove it?" Joe asked. "I mean, was there anyone with you who can back up your statement?"

"No. I was alone," Roger answered.

"What about your father?" Frank put in. "Didn't he see you?"

"He was visiting friends till late. I was already in bed when he got home."

"For your sake," Joe remarked, "I hope you're telling the truth."

Roger suddenly hurled his paintbrush to the ground. His face was flushed with anger. "I've had enough of you two!" he rasped. "What I do is none of your business!"

"We're making it our business," Joe told him.

Frank wanted to avoid a scene. "Simmer down," he said calmly. "We'll have to take your word for what you told us. But if you should run across any information concerning the theft, I advise you not to keep it to yourself."

The Hardys walked back to the convertible and returned to Bayport. Their mother and aunt were disappointed to see that the boys' father had not come with them.

"I suppose he's chasing after some horrible criminal!" Aunt Gertrude remarked. "Your father won't remember where he lives if he keeps up this sort of thing."

"Now calm down, Gertrude," Mrs Hardy pleaded in a soft voice.

Joe playfully sniffed the air. "Smells like roast turkey for supper."

"And coconut-custard pie for dessert," announced Mrs Hardy.

"Let's hope your sons can stay put long enough to eat it," said Aunt Gertrude.

The boys went to bed early that night. They spent the next day puttering around their crime lab and mulling over the case. It was mid afternoon when their father telephoned with an urgent message.

"Mr Alden just received another call from the thieves," said the detective. "He was told that the proof he had asked for would be found in a book entitled *Famous Horses of the World*, at the Clayton Library. Meet us there just as soon as you can."

The boys started out immediately. At the library they found their father and Alden seated at one of the reading tables examining a large book.

Mr Hardy handed his sons a photograph. "This was tucked in between the pages," he whispered.

The boys' eyes widened with surprise. "It's a picture of Topnotch," Frank said.

"Are you absolutely sure?" Joe asked.

"No doubt about it," Alden replied in a low voice.

"And it's a cul-de-sac when it comes to getting a line on who placed the photograph in the book," Mr Hardy said. "I questioned the librarian, but she has been too busy to take note of any strangers."

"May we keep the picture for a while?" Frank queried. "It might provide us with a clue."

"You're welcome to it," Alden replied. He glanced at his watch. "I'd better get back to the plant. The thieves will surely call me again."

Mr Hardy explained that Alden had had one of his drivers bring them to the library. He turned to the executive. "Why don't you send him back to the plant?

You and I can go along with the boys in their car."

"Very well," Alden agreed.

As they drove, Mr Hardy urged his client to stall for more time. "Tell those crooks that you can't get the ransom money until Friday morning," he said.

"I'll try." Alden sighed. "But I don't want to endanger Topnotch any more than I have to."

Soon the plant came into view. As they drove towards the main gate, Alden's experimental racing car suddenly sped out of the driveway.

"I didn't give anyone permission to drive that car!" he shouted.

Frank pressed down on the accelerator and the convertible shot off in pursuit!

·10·

Suspicious Rendezvous

"THAT racer is too fast for us!" Joe yelled. "We'll never catch it."

"Turn on to that side road just ahead!" Alden ordered. "We might be able to head him off!"

Frank followed instructions. It was a wild, bumpy ride and kept the occupants hanging on to their seats. After a couple of miles, the route led them back to the road along which their quarry was travelling.

"There's the experimental car!" Mr Hardy called excitedly, as he peered out of the rear window. "It's about a quarter of a mile behind us and coming fast!"

Frank skilfully manœuvred his convertible to prevent the other driver from passing.

"Hang on!" he cried out. "I'm going to start slowing down!"

As the Hardy car came to a stop, the other driver was forced to do the same.

"Good work!" Alden exclaimed, and leaped out of the convertible. The Hardys followed.

"Roger!" Joe exclaimed, as a sandy-haired young man slowly emerged from the experimental dragster.

Alden was furious. "What do you think you're doing?" he demanded.

"I—I was just taking your car for a little spin," his son stammered.

"Why aren't you working at the stable?" Alden fumed.

"I took the afternoon off," Roger replied.

Alden glared at his son with a look that would have melted ice. "You know my racer is a secret project. How dare you take it for a drive?"

He turned to the Hardys. "I'll meet you back at my office. I'm going to ride to the plant with Roger just to make sure he doesn't get any more wild ideas."

The Hardys reached the office just as Alden finished reprimanding his son.

"Don't send me away to that lumber camp," Roger was pleading.

"I don't see what else I can do with you," his father replied. "I'm fed up with your irresponsibility!"

"But I promise to stick with my job at the stable," Roger replied, "and I won't go near your experimental car again."

Alden rubbed his chin dubiously for a moment. "Well—all right," he finally agreed. "But step out of line once more and off you go."

Roger thanked his father. Then he rushed past the Hardys and out of the office.

At that instant the telephone rang. Alden picked it up. From his expression the Hardys knew it was another call from the thieves.

"Yes, I saw the photograph of Topnotch you placed in the book at the library," Alden informed the stranger. . . . "Will I pay the ransom you demand? I suppose I'll have to. But you must give me until

Friday. It'll take me that long to get such a large sum of money."

When the telephone conversation ended, Alden glanced at the Hardys. "They've agreed to wait till noon on Friday. I'm to receive further instructions then."

Frank jumped up. "That gives us two and a half days tó find out who stole your horse."

"We'll get to work on it right away," Mr Hardy said.

"I hope you're successful," Alden commented. "Fifty thousand dollars is a lot of money. But I'll pay it if I have to."

The Hardys hurried home to Bayport. There the elder detective began going through his criminal files. "I'll check to see if I have information on anyone whose speciality is horse-thieving," he said.

Meanwhile, his sons hurried off to their crime lab and studied the photograph of Topnotch.

"What are we looking for?" Joe inquired.

"I thought we might find something in the picture that would help us identify the locality," Frank replied.

"Slim chance. Other than the horse, there's nothing but a few bits of shrubbery."

"Wait a minute! That's it! Perhaps a botanist could tell us if the shrubs are indigenous to a particular region."

"Let's call Mr Scath, curator of the Howard Museum."

Frank rushed to the phone and dialled a number. Soon he had the curator on the line.

"We recently added a botanist to our staff," Scath

said. "His name is Mr Ronald Clause. I'm sure he can be of help to you."

"Would it be possible to see him right away?" Frank asked. "It's urgent."

"Yes," the curator assured him. "We're about to close the museum for the day, but Mr Clause plans to be here for a couple of hours to work on a new exhibit. I'll tell him you're coming."

The boys hurried to their car and drove to the museum, located in the north-western section of Bayport. A lanky, scholarly-looking man admitted them.

"I'm Mr Clause," he announced. "Mr Scath said you wanted to see me."

The boys introduced themselves, then stated their business. They handed the botanist the photograph of Topnotch.

"Hm! The shrubs are a bit out of focus," Clause muttered, "but I'll see what I can do."

"We realize you're very busy," Frank said. "However, we're racing against time. We'd appreciate it if you could give us an answer as soon as possible."

"I'll get to work on it right away," the botanist answered. "Might take me a day or so. If I come up with something, I'll call you."

The Hardys thanked him and left. As they drove back home, Frank's thoughts returned to Alden's son.

"I'm still not convinced that Roger had nothing to do with the theft of Topnotch," he remarked.

"I'm not either," Joe added. "Say, why don't we shadow him tomorrow? If he is in with the crooks, he might try to contact them."

"We've nothing to lose," Frank agreed. "But it

would be safer to have Roger shadowed by someone he doesn't know. That eliminates us and Chet."

"What about Biff Hooper and Tony Prito?" Joe suggested. "They've done a good job of following suspects for us before."

"Good idea. Let's call them when we get home."

Like Chet, Biff Hooper and Tony Prito were classmates of the boys at Bayport High. They always welcomed a chance to work with the Hardys on their cases.

"What's up?" Biff asked eagerly, as he and Tony joined the Hardys in their crime lab. "From your telephone call, I'd say it was important."

"It is," Frank assured him. "And we need your help."

Tony Prito, a dark-haired, lively boy, declared, "Count me in!"

Frank and Joe gave their friends a quick rundown on the case, then furnished them with a description of Roger.

"We'd like you to shadow him and give us a report on everything he does," Joe said.

"You'll find Roger at the stable in the morning," Frank added. "Try to be as inconspicuous as possible. We don't want him to suspect he's being watched."

Biff, a tall, blond, athletic-looking youth, beamed with enthusiasm. "You can depend on us!" he exclaimed.

The next day the Hardy boys stayed close to the telephone. It was almost one o'clock in the afternoon when a call came. Frank answered.

The caller was Biff Hooper. "Tony and I followed

your suspect to a restaurant in Clayton. He's inside talking to a couple of suspicious-looking characters."

"Are you calling from the restaurant?"

"No. I'm in a public phone booth across the street from it, on the corner of Stanton and Winthrop streets."

"Joe and I will come there right away!" Frank declared. "If Roger leaves in the meantime, stick with him. You can let us know where you are by leaving a message with Mother or Aunt Gertrude. We'll check with them every fifteen minutes."

The boys leaped into their car and headed for Clayton. When they arrived, Biff and Tony were still at their posts across the street from the restaurant.

"Your suspect hasn't left yet," Biff said.

Frank pointed to a building behind him. "Let's hide in that doorway, Joe," he advised. "We don't want Roger to spot us when he comes out."

The Hardys and their companions became impatient as the minutes ticked by. Finally Roger emerged from the restaurant with two rough-looking men. Each of them walked off in a different direction.

Frank turned to Biff. "You and Tony follow Roger," he ordered. "Joe and I will split up and trail those two men he was with."

Each boy hurried off on his assignment. Frank trailed his quarry for several blocks. Suddenly the man darted into an alley.

"He must know he's being followed," the young detective thought, and cautiously stalked towards the spot. He peered into the alley. There was nothing in it but a pile of discarded wooden crates at the far end.

"That man must be hiding behind them," Frank decided.

As he edged his way forward, the man leaped from behind the crates and flung a small object towards Frank. It hit the ground a few feet from the boy and exploded!

·11·

A Prize Catch

A THICK, white cloud of smoke erupted from the spot. Frank felt a burning sensation in his eyes and began to cough uncontrollably.

"It's tear gas," he thought. "I must get out of here!"

Frank stumbled backwards away from the smoke. At that instant he saw the blurred figure of a man running past him. The young detective lashed out with his fist and made contact. Then someone grabbed his left arm. Again Frank lashed out with his fist, but his punch was blocked.

"Hold it!" came the voice of his brother. "It's Joe!"

As the effects of the tear gas wore off, Frank saw a man lying unconscious on the ground. Joe pointed at the prone figure. "Looks as if you got your man," he said. "Wish I could say the same."

"You lost the other guy?" Frank asked.

"I had to let him go. He led me round the block and down this street past the alley. Then the smoke attracted my attention and I saw you were in trouble. So I ran to help."

The man regained consciousness. "Who—who are you guys?" he groaned as he struggled to his feet.

"Never mind that," Frank answered. "Suppose you tell us who *you* are?"

"My name's Marty Tempson, if it's any of your business," the man growled.

"Why did you toss that tear-gas bomb at me?"

"I thought you were some guy out to rob me."

"What kind of business did you and your pal have with Roger Alden?" Joe shot at him.

Tempson glared at the boys. "Roger Alden? I don't know no guy by that name," he snarled.

"You're lying," Frank declared. "He's the young man you and your friend were with in the restaurant."

"Never saw him before," Tempson replied. "The restaurant was crowded and he let us share his table."

At that moment a police patrol car arrived on the scene. One of the officers got out and approached the Hardys and Tempson.

"A shop owner across the street reported seeing smoke in this alley," the policeman announced. "What's going on here?"

The boys gave their names and Frank explained what had happened. When Tempson was unable to produce identification, the policeman searched him and discovered a tear-gas bomb in his pocket.

"I'm taking you in!" the officer declared.

Tempson turned pale. "You—you can't arrest me!" he stammered. "I ain't done nothing!"

"That's what you think," the policeman retorted. "There happens to be a law against tossing bombs at people." He glanced at the Hardys. "Will you come to the station and make a statement?"

"Glad to," Frank answered. "We'll pick up our car and meet you there."

Tempson was already being fingerprinted when the

boys arrived at Clayton Police Station. The desk sergeant took down their statement, then said that a complete check would be made on the prisoner.

"You boys must be in court when he's brought up for a preliminary hearing," the sergeant added. "That'll be tomorrow morning."

"We'll be here," Frank assured him.

He and Joe left the building and returned to their car.

"What's our next move?" Joe asked.

"Let's find out if Roger went back to the stable," Frank suggested. "If so, I want to question him."

Arriving at their destination, the boys found Roger seated in front of a stall repairing a harness. He was as belligerent as ever and became enraged when Frank declared that they had seen him in Clayton with two men.

"You lousy snoopers!" Roger yelled. "What right have you to spy on me?"

"Never mind that," Joe put in. "Who were the two men you were with?"

"I don't know," snapped the young man. "I went to the restaurant for lunch. The place was crowded and I let them share my table."

"Very considerate of you," Joe said sarcastically. "What made you so friendly all of a sudden?"

Roger jumped to his feet. "I don't have to take that from you!" he shouted.

In the next instant he swung the harness at Joe. The young detective stepped back, caught the end of the gear, then wrapped it tightly around his opponent's arms.

"Let me go!" Roger demanded.

"Not until you calm down!" Joe shot back.

Frank spoke up. "I don't think you're telling us the truth about not knowing those men."

"I am!" the young man cried out.

"Clayton is about ten miles north of here," Joe said. "Isn't that a long way to go just to have lunch? I've noticed a couple of local restaurants within walking distance."

"I like the food in Clayton," Roger replied mockingly.

"Why did you three walk off in different directions when you left the restaurant?" Frank questioned.

"I went my way, and they went theirs. How am I supposed to know where they were going?"

By now several grooms had collected round the boys. "Hey! Roger's wisecracking must have finally got him in trouble!" one of them yelled to his companion.

"Yeah! And he sure looks funny with that harness wrapped around him," another said, laughing. "I think he should keep it on permanently."

Joe felt a bit embarrassed and released Roger, who glared at the faces around him. Then he stormed off.

The Hardys headed back to Bayport. As they rode along, Joe said, "What do you think about Roger's story?"

"At least it tallies with what Tempson told us," Frank remarked. "But it could have been a pre-arranged alibi between him and the two men."

"If you ask me, there's something fishy about the whole thing."

When the boys got home, they went directly to their father's study.

"Glad to see you're back," Mr Hardy said. "Detective Tanner of the Clayton police telephoned a few minutes ago. He wants to talk to you two."

"What about?" Joe inquired.

"Marty Tempson. Tanner told me all about the tear-gas incident," their father replied. "They checked up on him. Seems his name is not Tempson, but Marty Seegan. He's wanted in Michigan for robbery."

"Then it means that Seegan will be extradited," Frank remarked, "and we won't have a chance to talk to him."

"Afraid so," Mr Hardy commented. "Since the Clayton police are holding Seegan on a lesser charge, the Michigan authorities get first crack at him. I was also asked to tell you," the detective continued, "that the preliminary hearing scheduled in the morning is off."

At that moment the telephone rang. Mr Hardy answered it. "It's for you, Frank."

"This is Mr Clause of the Howard Museum," the caller announced. "I have some information concerning the shrubbery you asked me to identify in the photograph."

· 12 ·

Startling Lead

"WHAT did you find out?" Frank asked him quickly.

"I've identified the shrubs as *Rubus Diparitus*," Clause told him. "They're indigenous to Maryland and parts of Virginia."

Frank thanked the botanist for his help. He then informed his brother and Mr Hardy about Clause's discovery.

"Maryland!" Joe exclaimed. "That's a coincidence. Aunt Gertrude's stable is located there."

"Let's go and see Mr Fowler, the manager, first thing in the morning," Frank suggested. "Maybe he can help us find Topnotch. Is it all right if we have Jack Wayne fly us there, Dad?"

"Sure, boys."

Jack Wayne, a tanned, lean-faced man, was the pilot of Mr Hardy's personal single-engine plane. The boys telephoned him and requested that he be ready for an early departure the next day. Dawn was just breaking as Jack began his take-off roll at the Bayport field.

"Too bad Dad couldn't come with us," Joe remarked, as he watched the ground drop away beneath them.

"Yes," Frank agreed, "but he wants to be within reach of Mr Alden if something should come up."

It took little more than an hour to reach their

destination. Jack landed the plane on a small field about four miles from Aunt Gertrude's stable. The airport operator, a genial man, lent the Hardys a car which he kept for the convenience of visitors.

"We might be gone for several hours," Frank told the pilot.

"Don't worry about me," Jack said. "I'll stick around here and do some hangar flying with the fellows."

As soon as the boys arrived at Southern Pines Stables, they spotted a short, wiry man standing in front of one of the stalls. His hard features and deep-set eyes gave him a forbidding appearance.

"We'd like to see Mr Fowler," Joe informed him.

"Whatcha want to see 'im about?" the man asked in a raspy voice.

"It's confidential," Frank said. "We'd appreciate it if you would tell us where we can find him."

The man stared coldly at the boys for a moment. Then he pointed towards a knoll in the distance. "You'll find 'im on the other side of that hill. He's practice shootin' with his rifle."

The muffled sound of rifle shots could be heard in the distance. Frank thanked the man and the boys started off. As they crossed over the crest of the hill, they spotted Fowler at the bottom of a shallow gully. He was firing at a paper target.

"Well, if it isn't the Hardys!" Fowler called out, when he saw them approaching. "What brings you to this neck of the woods? Business?"

"Not exactly," Frank replied. He then told the manager about the theft of Alden's race horse.

"Why are you telling me all this?" Fowler snapped. "I've never heard of Topnotch."

"We're pretty sure that the horse is being kept somewhere here in Maryland or Virginia," Joe explained. "You must come in contact with lots of stable owners. We thought you might have heard rumours that . . ."

"Sorry! Can't help you," the manager interrupted. "Maryland and Virginia cover a lot of territory. That horse could be anywhere." He squeezed off a couple of shots, then turned to the Hardys. "I regret I can't spend more time with you, but I've lots of work to do. I'm sure you understand."

As the boys followed Fowler out of the gully, Frank picked up one of the spent cartridge cases from the manager's rifle. He quickly stuck it into his pocket.

A few minutes later they were back at the stable. The short, wiry man the boys talked to when they first arrived was nowhere in sight.

"Sorry to cut your visit so short," Fowler said, shaking hands with the young detectives. "Come again when I'm not tied up."

The boys walked back to their car.

"Fowler was certainly in a hurry to get rid of us," Joe commented. "He acted mighty suspicious. Why don't we stick around and see what's going on?"

"No. We're flying back to Bayport right away," Frank announced. "If my hunch is right, we'll save a lot of time in our investigation."

"What hunch?"

Frank dipped into his pocket and pulled out the cartridge case he had picked up. "This shell is of the same calibre as the one we found the day the smoke bomb was fired into Dad's study," he said. "But I can't tell whether it was fired from the same rifle until I make a microscopic comparison."

"Leaping lizards!" Joe exclaimed. "If they do check out, it would connect Fowler with the gang that's after Alden's experimental motor!"

"And the same gang might have stolen Topnotch," Frank added.

Soon the boys and their pilot were winging back to Bayport.

Mrs Hardy greeted her sons when they arrived home. "I didn't expect you so soon. Your father left on an errand a few minutes ago. Then he's going directly to Mr Alden's home. He told me he can be reached there in about two hours."

The boys hurried to their crime lab. Frank took the first cartridge case he had found, and placed it with the second in the comparison microscope. He peered into the eyepieces of the apparatus for several minutes.

"What's the verdict?" Joe asked impatiently.

Suddenly Frank leaped to his feet. "My hunch has paid off!" he exclaimed. "Take a look! The markings on the cartridges match exactly!"

"Wait till Dad hears this!"

Frank glanced at his watch. "Let's drive to Alden's home," he suggested. "Dad should be there by the time we arrive."

The boys dashed to their car. An hour went by before they pulled into a driveway leading to a large, white house. It was set back from the road on a spacious, tree-covered lawn.

An elderly servant responded to a single press of the doorbell. "What can I do for you?" he asked.

"We're Mr Hardy's sons," Joe explained. "We must see our father right away."

"Oh, yes," the servant answered, as he pulled the door open all the way. "He arrived with Mr Alden a few minutes ago. Please come in."

The boys were ushered into Alden's study. Mr Hardy was surprised to see them.

"Back from Maryland already?" he said. "Have any luck."

"You bet!" Frank replied excitedly.

Their father and Mr Alden listened with interest as the two boys told them about their startling lead.

The executive sat bolt upright in his chair. "If what you suspect about this man Fowler is true," he said, "then we must do something right away."

"I'm going to call Chief Collig," Mr Hardy declared. He dialled a number and shortly had the officer on the line.

"Those cartridge cases are strong evidence," the chief remarked, when told about Fowler. "I'll contact the Maryland State Police and have him picked up for questioning. You should hear from me within a couple of hours."

Alden arranged to have dinner served while they waited. Nearly three hours passed before the phone rang. Mr Hardy rushed to pick it up.

"This is Chief Collig," the caller said. "Looks like your suspect flew the coop. The Maryland police went to the stable and found no one around."

"In that case, will you issue an APB on him?" Mr

Hardy asked. "Frank and Joe can give you a detailed description of Fowler."

"I'll send it out immediately," Collig assured him.

Frank got on the phone and furnished the police chief with the necessary information. Then he and his companions mulled over the situation.

"No wonder Fowler was eager to get rid of us," Joe muttered. "He was planning a getaway. But we still don't know if he had anything to do with the theft of Topnotch."

Frank was casually gazing at some photographs mounted on the wall of the study. Suddenly his eyes widened in amazement.

"I—I don't believe it!" he shouted.

·13·

No Trespassing!

"WHAT is it?" Joe asked, surprised at Frank's outburst.

Frank pointed to a photograph showing a small group of men. "Take a look at the face of the man standing next to Mr Alden in this picture," he urged.

Joe peered at the photograph in astonishment. "Why—it's Fowler!" he exclaimed.

"The picture you're looking at was taken three years ago during a fishing trip I went on with some friends," Alden interjected as he gazed at the boys curiously. "That man's name is not Fowler. It's Norman Dodson. He's a distant cousin of mine."

"I'm sure we're not mistaken," Frank insisted. "He's the suspect we're after!"

"The idea is utterly ridiculous," the executive countered. "Why would Norman get mixed up with a gang of crooks? He—"

"Think back," Mr Hardy interrupted. "Did you and Dodson ever have a quarrel in the past?"

There was a momentary pause.

"As a matter of fact we did," Alden said finally. "About a year ago."

"What happened?" Frank asked.

"Norman was once a junior partner in my firm," the

executive explained. "However, he became more interested in the raising of race horses than in automobiles. One day he asked to be bought out so that he could purchase a stable. Unfortunately, his venture failed and Norman lost his money."

"The pieces are beginning to fit together," Joe observed.

"Then about a year ago," Alden continued, "he came to my office and demanded more money. He said that I hadn't paid him enough for his share in the firm. I refused, and we had a bitter argument. I haven't seen him since."

"No doubt about it!" Frank declared. "Dodson must have masterminded the theft of Topnotch. And his motive is clear. He's out to get more money from you one way or another."

"I still find it hard to believe," Alden sighed.

The Hardys returned to Bayport. Aunt Gertrude went into a frenzy when she heard about Topnotch and their suspect. "My stable is not only a haven for retired race horses," she cried, "but for stolen ones as well!"

"Let's call Mr Steve Benson, attorney for the estate," Frank suggested to his father. "He should be able to give us more information on Dodson."

Frank dialled the number. It took only seconds to reach the lawyer in Maryland. Benson was shocked to hear about the missing stable manager. He stated that Fowler had worked several months for the previous owner before their aunt inherited the business.

"But I only knew him by the name of Fowler," Benson added. "He was the most competent of all the workers there. When I was placed in charge of the estate I made him temporary manager."

"Is there anything else you can tell us about him?" Frank asked.

"Only that he was interested in buying the stable when he learned it was for sale," the lawyer said. "However, he was unable to raise the cash. Later he asked if I would help him sell a piece of land that he owned."

"A piece of land?" Frank blurted. "Where?"

"In northern Vermont," Benson replied. "He showed me the exact spot on a road map. It consists of about twenty acres and a cabin. But I wasn't really interested in handling the matter."

Frank quickly obtained a map of Vermont. He then asked the attorney to describe where Fowler's land was located. Benson stated that it was just west of Highway 15, twelve miles north of the town of Haversville.

After Frank had hung up, he said, "I'll bet Fowler-Dodson has gone to his cabin!"

"It would be a perfect place to hide out with Top-notch," Joe agreed. "But wouldn't he be taking a big chance? After all, he told Mr Benson where his land was located."

"Dodson might be hoping the attorney forgot about it, or wouldn't think it important enough to mention," Mr Hardy said.

"How about requesting the police up there to check the area?" Frank spoke up. "It's been more than fourteen hours since we last saw Dodson. He could easily be in Vermont by now."

Mr Hardy telephoned Chief Collig again. Two

hours passed before the Bayport officer called back.

"A couple of officers searched the cabin and some of the surrounding land," he informed the detective. "Afraid you're out of luck. They found nothing."

"Thanks, Chief," Mr Hardy replied. "By the way, our suspect would have to transport Topnotch in a horse van. Would you send out an alarm to have all such vehicles—spotted within a six- or seven-hundred-mile radius—stopped and inspected? Although I'm sure it's too late for that now."

"I'll do it, anyway," the chief assured him.

"Guess we've run into another blank wall," Joe muttered.

"Not necessarily," Frank commented. He snapped his fingers. "Let's go to Vermont and take a look ourselves. Dodson's pretty clever. He certainly wouldn't keep Topnotch there at the cabin. It's possible he's hiding somewhere nearby."

"I'm with you," his brother said.

"Go to it," Mr Hardy told them. "I'll have to stay behind and sit it out with Mr Alden. Remember! Noon tomorrow is the deadline for him to pay the ransom."

The boys alerted Jack Wayne for another flight the next morning. After an early breakfast, they drove to the airport and boarded the plane.

"Flight time should be approximately two and a half hours," the pilot announced. "The nearest field is about twenty miles from where you want to go."

Jack's estimated time to reach their destination proved to be correct. After landing, the Hardys arranged to rent a car.

"You stick close to the phone here in operations," Frank instructed Jack. "If you don't hear from us in two hours, notify the police."

"Roger," Jack replied. "Good luck!"

Soon Frank and Joe were driving north on Highway 15. When they were twelve miles north of Haversville, they spotted a crude fence a few yards west of the road. On it was a large sign which read:

PRIVATE PROPERTY
NO TRESPASSING

"This must be Dodson's land," Joe concluded.

Frank turned the car on to a narrow, dirt trail which jutted off the highway. After travelling a short distance, he brought it to a stop.

"We'd better continue on foot," he advised.

The Hardys picked their way through an area of dense woods and brush. Soon they came to a small clearing.

"There's the cabin!" Joe declared, pointing to a dilapidated log structure directly ahead.

"Let's watch it from here for a while," Frank said. "There might be someone inside."

Half an hour went by. There was no sign of life, and the only sound was that of the wind rustling through the trees.

"I think it's safe to go in," Joe remarked impatiently.

"Okay. Let's go!"

They skirted the clearing and approached the cabin from the rear. When they reached it, Frank cautiously peered through a window.

"The place is empty except for a couple of pieces of furniture," he told his brother.

The boys walked round to the front of the cabin and climbed two steps to the porch.

"Careful," Frank warned. "These planks are pretty creaky. Step lightly."

The door of the cabin did not have a lock. The boys pushed it open and went inside. A wooden table stood in the middle of the floor with worn-out chairs set at each end. Suspended from the ceiling above the table was an old paraffin lamp.

Joe walked over to a cupboard mounted against the wall. He pulled open the door. "Look at this!" he exclaimed. "A supply of tinned food!"

Frank inspected his brother's discovery. "These tins look as if they haven't been here long. No dust on them."

Suddenly the boys heard the voices of men in the distance.

"Someone's coming!" Joe said excitedly. "Sounds as if they're approaching from the woods behind the cabin."

"Let's get out of here!" Frank said.

The boys dashed through the door and across the clearing to the edge of the woods. They took cover in a clump of thick brush. A moment later three men appeared from round the corner of the cabin.

"That tall guy is the one I trailed from the restaurant in Clayton," Joe whispered.

"And we met the short one at the Southern Pines Stables when we went to see Dodson," Frank hissed.

Neither of the Hardys recognized the third man, who

remarked, "Dodson would nail us to a wall if he knew we came to the cabin!"

"I'm hungry," another said. "I can't wait till dark to get some of that tinned food!"

The three men hurried into the log structure and slammed the door behind them.

"I'm going back to try to hear what they're saying," Joe announced.

"It's too risky in daylight," his brother warned.

But Joe was already on his way. Frank watched him sprint across the clearing and carefully step up on to the porch of the cabin.

Suddenly there was a loud cracking sound. Frank's pulse quickened. "Some of the planks are giving way underneath Joe!" he thought.

The next instant there was a crash as Joe fell through the porch floor up to his waist. Frank rushed to his aid. As he reached his brother, the three men spilled out of the cabin!

·14·

Daring Escape

THERE was a violent struggle. Frank lashed out at one of the men and sent him hurtling back into the cabin. The remaining two pounced on the dark-haired youth.

"Run for it!" Joe shouted, as he frantically tried to free himself from between the planks.

One of Frank's assailants caught him from behind with a headlock. The young detective flipped him high over his shoulder in judo fashion.

"Hold it!" came an order. Frank suddenly found himself staring into the face of Dodson, who patted a rear pocket significantly.

"Er—hi, Boss," one of the men said nervously. "We came to get some tinned food and caught a couple of snoopers."

"What did I tell you guys about coming here in daylight?" Dodson yelled. He glared at the Hardys. "How did you know where to find me?"

"Trade secret," Joe snapped, as he finally worked himself free of the planks and rejoined his brother.

"These kids probably told somebody they were coming here!" Dodson said to his cohorts. "We'd better move the horse van to another hiding place."

"But what about the ransom money?" said one of the men. "Kurt will be comin' here after he picks it up."

Dodson looked at his watch. "It's early yet. He'll still be in his room at the hotel in Clayton." He turned to the short, wiry man the boys had met at the Southern Pines Stables. "Beaver! Get to a telephone and call Kurt. Tell him to go ahead as planned, then to drive to the bus terminal in Haversville. We'll meet him there tonight."

"Okay, Boss," Beaver replied, as he hurried off.

The boys were ordered to walk ahead of their captors.

"Where are you taking us?" Frank demanded.

"You two went to a lot of trouble to find Topnotch," Dodson snarled. "I'm going to give you a chance to see him."

The Hardys were marched along what appeared to be a very narrow trail through the woods. Actually they saw it was a wide, dirt road, cleverly covered with brush.

Soon the boys were ordered to halt. A huge mound of dried brush loomed in front of them. One of their captors pulled it aside.

"Why—it's a camouflage net," Joe whispered to his brother.

"And it's covering a horse van," Frank answered in a low voice.

"Shut up!" Dodson demanded. "Get inside!"

The boys walked up a ramp which formed the rear door of the van when closed. To the right in the back of the van was a small bedroom for the trainer. Ahead, another door with bars at the top opened into a stall. Inside was Topnotch who began to whinny at the disturbance.

Frank and Joe were roughly pushed into the van. A quick glimpse at the race horse revealed that his distinguishing white marks above the front hoofs had been dyed chestnut to match his coat.

"This animal," Dodson remarked with a laugh, "has been living like a king. After all, he means fifty thousand dollars to me."

"You won't get away with this!" Joe vowed.

"Who's going to stop me?" Dodson retorted. He then barked an order to his pals. "Tie these wise guys up!" His henchman shoved the boys inside the small room and uncoiled lengths of rope.

"No use resisting," Frank told Joe. He winked. "Just relax." Joe nodded in response.

As they were being tied up, the boys took deep breaths and flexed their muscles hard. The men wound the ropes tightly round the boys' bodies, then they left with Dodson. The rear door was slammed shut.

Instantly the Hardys exhaled and relaxed their muscles. The ropes went slack and the boys had little difficulty freeing themselves.

"Thanks for reminding me to relax," Joe said with a grin. "I had almost forgotten that old trick Dad taught us."

"We're lucky Dodson's men don't know much about tying up prisoners," Frank remarked.

A scraping sound outside told the boys that their captors were removing the camouflage net covering the van.

"They're getting ready to move," Frank said. "We must get out of here fast!"

"Let's make a break for it! It's our only chance."

Dodson's henchmen tied the ropes tightly round the Hardy boys

The boys dashed from the small room, but were dismayed to find the door of the van locked.

"There's no other exit!" Joe said frantically.

"I have an idea!" Frank whispered. "We'll ride Topnotch out of here!"

"What! Through a locked door?"

"We'll force Dodson and his men to open it!"

"How?"

"By raising such a racket that they'll let down the door to investigate."

The boys opened the door to the stall, patted the horse, who seemed to recognize them, then bridled him. Quickly they lead Topnotch to within a few feet of the rear door.

"Hey!" came the voice of one of their captors. "Do you hear Topnotch movin' around?"

"Probably just restless," Dodson replied. "He'll calm down."

Frank leaned close to Joe. "All set?" he whispered.

His brother nodded, and the boys began pounding on the door with their fists.

"What's that?" they heard a man shout. "It's comin' from inside the van."

"Maybe the kids got loose!" Dodson declared. "We'd better check. Quick! Open the door!"

The Hardys leaped on to Topnotch and flattened out on his back. As the ramp was pulled down, they nudged the racehorse forward. He sprinted down the ramp, taking the men completely by surprise. Before they could recover, Topnotch had covered a hundred yards.

"They're getting away!" one of the men yelled.

Suddenly Topnotch stumbled and the Hardys were thrown to the ground. They scrambled to their feet just in time to see Dodson take a small object from his pocket and throw it towards them.

"Looks like a tear-gas bomb!" Frank yelled.

Joe darted ahead and caught the object, then tossed it back at their captors. On contact with the ground, the bomb exploded and engulfed Dodson and his henchmen in a thick, white cloud of smoke.

As the choking gas began to drift away, the boys, holding their breaths, pounced on them and wrestled the men into the van. They shut and locked the door.

Joe glanced around. "Where's Topnotch?"

"He ran off!" Frank said. "You stay on guard here. I'll go and look for him."

After a brief search Frank found the horse behind a clump of trees, entangled in heavy brush. He freed him and led the animal back to the van.

At that moment the Hardys were startled to hear their names called. "Frank! Joe! Where are you?"

"Sounds like Jack Wayne," Joe said. "He must be at the cabin."

Frank sprinted down the brush-covered trail. Reaching the clearing, he saw the pilot and two state troopers standing near the cabin.

"Jack!" Frank shouted, as he ran to greet them.

"Am I glad to see you!" Jack said, with a sigh of relief. "I jumped the gun a bit. Didn't quite wait out a full two hours. Thought you'd call me long before that. I began to worry and notified the State Police."

"Glad you did." Frank told Jack and the officers what had happened, then led them to the van.

"You're under arrest!" one of the troopers announced as the boys pulled the door of the vehicle down. Dodson and his henchmen staggered out and were handcuffed.

"There was a fourth man with them," Joe put in. "He went to make a call."

"Where's the nearest telephone?" Frank asked the officers.

"There's a public booth about a mile and a half down the highway," one of them replied.

Frank checked his watch. "Let's drive in that direction," he suggested. "Beaver was on foot. He should be on his way back by now."

"We'll use the patrol car," one of the troopers said, and added, "I'll have to radio headquarters for more help."

Leaving Jack and the other officer behind to guard the prisoners, the Hardys and their companion hurried to the highway. Soon they were cruising in the patrol car.

Minutes later, Joe pointed to a wiry figure trekking back along the highway. "There he is! That's Beaver!"

The officer brought the car to an abrupt halt and leaped out, with the boys close at his heels.

"What—what's this?" Beaver shouted as he was placed under arrest. "How did you kids escape?"

"Save your breath," Joe snapped. "You'll soon have enough talking to do."

It was not long before more troopers arrived on the scene. Two grooms from a nearby stable were summoned to take charge of Topnotch until his owner could claim him.

Dodson and his cohorts were driven to Haversville Police Headquarters. There Frank telephoned Alden's plant.

"Sorry," said the executive's secretary, "but Mr Alden and Mr Hardy left a few minutes ago on urgent business. I don't know when they'll return."

"They're probably on their way to pay the ransom money," Frank remarked as he hung up.

"The guy named Kurt is in for a surprise when he arrives at the bus terminal tonight," Joe commented with a grin. "He'll have quite a reception party waiting for him."

"You can say that again," Frank said. He then turned to their pilot. "Jack, fly back to Bayport and keep trying to contact Dad and Mr Alden. When you do, bring them here."

"Okay."

The Hardys interrogated the prisoners but without success. After an early dinner at a restaurant in town they returned to police headquarters. They were elated to find their father waiting for them.

"Just got here," Mr Hardy said. "Heard you boys cracked the horse-thieving case. Good work."

"Thanks, Dad," Frank answered. "Where's Mr Alden? Didn't he come with you?"

"He intended to. But just as we were leaving his office, he received word that Roger was involved in an automobile accident," the detective explained. "Jack went back to Bayport and will fly Mr Alden here in the morning if Roger isn't seriously hurt."

"What about the ransom?" Joe asked.

"Mr Alden decided to pay it," his father replied.

"He received a call precisely at noon today and was instructed to leave the money in a public locker at the Clayton railroad station. I wanted to stick around and try to nab the pickup man, but Mr Alden wouldn't hear of it. He was afraid of losing Topnotch if anything went wrong."

The boys told him about Kurt.

"This is a great piece of luck!" Mr Hardy exclaimed.

Frank glanced at his watch. "If Kurt picked up the money and departed from Clayton by one o'clock this afternoon, he should reach Haversville about ten or eleven o'clock tonight."

As the hour neared, the three Hardys posted themselves across the street from the bus terminal. Several plainclothesmen were assigned to accompany them.

The time ticked by slowly. It was almost midnight before a car approached and parked in front of the terminal building. A burly man climbed out.

"That could be our man," Mr Hardy whispered.

"Trouble is, we don't know what Kurt looks like," Joe muttered.

Frank was struck with an idea. He stepped out of the shadows and nonchalantly walked towards their suspect. "Hi, Kurt!" he said.

The man whirled. "Hi! Er—who are you?" he responded with a startled expression.

"You're under arrest!" the young detective declared.

The man tried to make a break for it, but Frank seized him. Plainclothesmen closed in from all sides.

"What is this?" their captive shouted. "I ain't done nothin'."

"We know who you are!" Frank shot back.

"Where's the ransom money?" Mr Hardy demanded.

"What money?" Kurt sputtered.

"It's probably in his car," Joe put in. He quickly searched the vehicle and found a package stuffed underneath the front seat.

"That's it," Mr Hardy observed.

The prisoner was taken to police headquarters. There he was brought face to face with Dodson.

"Gosh, Boss," Kurt began, "I . . ."

"Shut up!" Dodson screamed. "Idiot! You walked straight into a trap!"

"But nobody warned me! How was I supposed to know?"

"As long as you're in the mood for talking," Frank spoke up, "suppose you answer a few questions."

"I told you before," Dodson retorted, "you're not getting anything out of me."

"Is there someone else in this with you?" Mr Hardy inquired.

A smirk spread across Dodson's face. "Why don't you ask Alden's son?"

· 15 ·

Plea for Help

"WHAT do you mean by that remark?" Frank demanded.

"You guys think you're so smart," Dodson snapped. "Figure it out for yourselves."

After the prisoners were escorted to their cells, the Hardys went to a local hotel to spend the night. The next morning Mr Alden and Jack Wayne arrived just as the boys and their father were finishing breakfast.

"You've done a terrific job," Alden said. "And I'm glad to know that Topnotch is all right."

"We've recovered the ransom money too," Joe announced.

"What!" Alden exclaimed. "That's incredible."

After a pause Mr Hardy inquired, "How's your son?"

"Fine, thank you. It was just a minor car accident, and I was happy to hear it wasn't his fault. Fortunately Roger escaped injury and reported for work at the stable this morning."

Frank said quietly, "We're sorry that your cousin is one of the thieves."

Alden also expressed some remorse for Dodson. He hinted that he might drop the charges against him.

"But you can't let him go free," Mr Hardy objected. "We've reason to suspect that your cousin is involved with someone who is trying to steal your experimental motor. He might turn out to be our only link."

Alden finally agreed.

Then the detective said, "We're going to take another crack at questioning Dodson before we fly back to Bayport. You'd better come to headquarters with us. The police will want a statement."

"All right." Alden sighed. "But please don't ask me to be at the interrogation. You understand. Anyway, I want to arrange to take Topnotch home today."

When Dodson was grilled by the Hardys, he continued to be unco-operative.

"You were the one who fired the smoke grenade into our father's study, weren't you?" Frank said.

"I don't know what you're talking about," Dodson insisted.

"No use denying it," Joe interjected. "We have evidence to prove that the grenade was fired from your rifle."

The prisoner nervously gripped the arms of his chair. "You're lying!" he screamed.

"Who's trying to steal Mr Alden's experimental motor?" Mr Hardy demanded.

"I don't know anything about a motor!" Dodson shouted. He jumped to his feet. "I want to go back to my cell!"

Shortly he was ushered out of the room. The Hardys then questioned each of the other prisoners in turn. But they too refused to talk. Obviously Dodson had frightened the men into remaining silent.

After lunch Jack Wayne flew the Hardys back to Bayport. When they arrived, Frank suggested that they drive to the stable near Alden's plant and tell Roger about Dodson's remark.

"I'd like to see what his reaction will be," Frank added.

"You boys go ahead. I must get back to another case," Mr Hardy told them. "I'll take a taxi home."

The boys hurried to the airport car park and climbed into their car. Soon they were at the stable confronting Roger with Dodson's insinuation.

"I barely know my father's cousin," the young man yelled. "He's crazy!"

"Then what reason would Dodson have for trying to involve you?" Frank asked.

Roger grew pale. "Don't ask me!" he retorted. "Maybe he's trying to get back at my father through me."

"Then you've nothing to worry about—if you're not involved," Joe said.

"Leave me alone!" The young man nervously fumbled with a bucket he was carrying. "Get out of here! I have work to do!"

"Okay," Frank replied. "But don't forget this. When Dodson and his gang are put on trial, your name is likely to pop up again. If so, the prosecutor will have you subpoenaed."

When the boys returned home, Chet Morton was waiting in the driveway with his bicycle.

"Hi, fellows!" Their friend was bubbling with excitement. "Long time no see!"

"Hello, Chet!" Frank said. "Why the bicycle? Car break down?"

"No," the plump youth answered. "Remember the

rocket cycle I told you I was going to design? Well, this is it!"

Frank and Joe noticed a square canister attached underneath the seat of the bicycle. A long, funnel-shaped nozzle protruded from it.

"Don't tell us it works," Joe said.

"I don't know yet," Chet admitted. "I wanted to wait until you master minds could be on hand to witness the supreme test."

"Forget it," Frank advised. "That thing looks dangerous."

Chet shrugged off the warning. He leaped on to the seat of the bicycle and flicked a small toggle switch mounted on the handle bar. A crackling sound came from the canister. Then suddenly a long tongue of flame shot out from the nozzle. Chet was carried off with a roar. He manœuvred the bicycle through several wide circles as its speed rapidly increased.

"Cut off the motor!" Joe cried anxiously.

"I—I can't!" their friend stammered.

In the next instant Chet steered on a straight course and vanished down the street in a trail of smoke. The Hardys jumped into their car and took off in pursuit.

"Where did he go?" Joe said anxiously, after they had travelled about half a mile.

"Look! Over there!"

Frank pointed to a bicycle, minus its rider, turned over on a spacious lawn. The wheels were still spinning.

"There's no sign of Chet," Joe muttered worriedly.

"I see him!" Frank declared.

He led his brother to a thick hedge a short distance away. Chet's legs were protruding from the top.

"Are you all right?" Joe yelled.

"Yes, I'm okay! Get me out of here!"

The boys pulled their chum free of the hedge. He was badly shaken by his experience, but other than a few scratches he had suffered no injuries.

"Better stick to the old-fashioned way of propelling a bike," Frank urged.

"Guess you're right." Chet sighed. "It wasn't such a good idea, anyway."

The Hardys drove their friend and his rocket bike to the Morton farm. Then they returned home in time to enjoy a delicious dinner. The meal was interrupted by the telephone. Frank answered it.

"This is Roger," the caller announced. He seemed frightened. "I've got to see you right away. But I don't want to come to your home. Meet me at the municipal car park in Bayport."

The boys quickly finished eating, then drove off to their rendezvous with Alden's son. They found him seated in his car. At Roger's request the boys climbed into the rear seat.

"What's this all about?" Frank demanded.

"You must help me," the young man pleaded.

"Help you?" Joe snapped. "Why should we?"

"I'm in terrible trouble," Roger said shakily. "I *was* in on the theft of Topnotch. But I didn't know the horse was to be held for ransom."

"Then why did you get involved?" Frank asked.

"I wanted revenge for the way my father has been treating me."

"How did you get mixed up with Dodson?" Joe questioned.

Roger stated that he met his father's cousin one night in Clayton. "I realize now that it was not a chance meeting. He must have followed me there after work. Said he'd heard I wasn't on friendly terms with my father. I never thought to ask him how he knew that."

"Hm! Interesting," Frank muttered.

"Dodson then told me that he also had a grudge against my father," Roger continued, "and asked me if I would like to play a joke on him."

"Like stealing Topnotch?" Joe interjected.

"Yes. But Dodson promised that the horse would be returned in a few days. It wasn't until they attacked the groom the night we took Topnotch that I realized the theft was meant to be more than a joke."

"Why did you meet two of Dodson's henchmen in that restaurant in Clayton?" Frank inquired. "By then you knew they were crooks."

"I had to," Roger replied. "Dodson sent them to warn me not to talk; otherwise he'd see that I went to jail with them."

"What made you change your mind?" Joe asked.

"When you told me Dodson had mentioned my name, I thought it over and decided to tell you what I know. I would have before, but I was afraid."

"You made a wise decision," Frank assured him. "And if you continue to co-operate, we'll do everything in our power to see that you get a break."

"What should I do now?" Roger asked.

"I suggest you tell your father everything you've told us," Frank advised. "You're going to need his help as well as ours."

Roger thanked the Hardys and drove off.

"Roger's completely changed," Joe commented, as he and his brother returned to their car.

"He's scared," Frank said. "And it's a good thing. Maybe this will teach him a lesson."

When the boys arrived home, their father greeted them with alarming news.

"Dodson has escaped!" he announced.

·16·

Dilemma

FRANK and Joe were startled by the news.

"I can't believe it!" Joe exclaimed.

"How did he manage to get away?" Frank asked quickly.

"That's the most fantastic part of what I have to tell you," Mr Hardy replied.

He told his sons that Lieutenant Monroe of the Haversville police had telephoned. The officer had informed him that Dodson escaped while he and his men were being transferred to the county jail in Myles City.

"The prisoners were sent in a patrol car," Mr Hardy continued. "When they were about halfway to their destination, the windshield suddenly crazed. The driver lost control, skidded off the road, and turned over in a ditch."

"Leaping lizards!" Joe exclaimed. "That's exactly what caused Mr Alden's racing cars to crash!"

"Then what happened?" Frank asked.

"The occupants were badly shaken up," the detective replied. "But one of the officers faintly recalls seeing two masked men run towards the patrol car. They pulled Dodson out and disappeared. That's all he remembers."

"What about the men with him?" Frank inquired.

"They were left behind," Mr Hardy answered.

"That's strange," Joe muttered. "I wonder why."

"I don't know," their father admitted. "But I suggest we fly to Myles City tomorrow and have another talk with Dodson's pals."

At that moment Aunt Gertrude entered the room and began one of her tirades.

"Horse-thieves! Ransom money! It's all too horrible to imagine," she sputtered. "And to think those criminals were connected with that awful stable I inherited."

"It's not really as bad as all that," Mrs Hardy commented in a soft voice. "Horses are wonderful animals. Think how pleasant it must be for them to have a lovely place to retire."

"Fiddlesticks!" Aunt Gertrude retorted. "I'll have no part of it." She glanced at Mr Hardy. "Are you sure Mr Benson is doing his best to sell the stable?"

"Yes, he is," the detective assured her. "You'll probably be hearing from him any day now."

"I certainly hope so," his sister said. "The next thing you know, they'll be setting up public ticket booths and holding races in the paddock."

The others smiled, then Frank changed the subject.

Early the next morning Jack Wayne and the Hardys were streaking down the runway on take-off at the Bayport field. Less than three hours later, the boys and their father were at the county jail in Myles City. Lieutenant Monroe was there to greet them.

"We've checked on the prisoners," he said. "They all have police records a mile long."

"We'd like to question them one at a time," Mr Hardy requested.

"Okay," the lieutenant replied. "We can use the chief guard's office."

Beaver was the only one among the three prisoners willing to talk. "Dodson's left us holding the bag!" he growled. "That rat won't get away with this. Whatcha' want to know?"

"When did you first meet Dodson?" Mr Hardy asked.

"A couple of months ago in Maryland," Beaver answered. "I was on the lam at the time and came across the stable he was managin'. He was lookin' for workers and offered me a job. I took it 'cause I thought it would be a good place to lay low for a while."

"Was it his idea to steal Topnotch?" Frank questioned.

"Yes," the prisoner admitted. "I got to be on friendly terms with Dodson. Told 'im I had a police record. He said not to worry about it. Later he asked me if I would help his men steal a race horse, and get a couple o' my friends to come in on the deal. Needin' money, I jumped at the chance."

"Do you know if he was involved in any other shady activities?" Joe asked.

"Not that I know of," Beaver replied. "But he was away from the stable two and three days at a stretch sometimes. Maybe he *was* up to somethin' that he never told me about."

"Think hard," Mr Hardy urged. "Did Dodson ever

mention anything about experimental racing cars or motors?"

"Not to me he didn't," the prisoner answered.

When the interview was over, the boys and their father discussed the information.

"I believe he was telling the truth," Frank commented.

"So do I," Mr Hardy agreed. "And it explains why Beaver and the other two prisoners were left behind."

"What do you mean?" Joe queried.

"I'm convinced that Dodson is part of a gang that's trying to steal Mr Alden's experimental motor. The theft of Topnotch must have been his own private deal. As a result, the gang knew nothing about his horse-theft plans or the men who were helping him."

"Makes sense," Joe remarked. He thought for a moment. "But how did the guys who helped him escape know he was being taken to Myles City?"

Frank turned to Lieutenant Monroe, who was seated nearby. "Did Dodson have any visitors, or make any phone calls from Haversville?" he asked.

"He didn't have any visitors," the officer told him, "but he was permitted to make a call. When I informed him that we were taking him to Myles City, he demanded that he be allowed to contact his lawyer. I dialled the number for him."

"Did you check the number?" Frank asked.

"No," the lieutenant replied. "But I have a record of it back at headquarters. I'll call the desk sergeant and have him check it immediately."

Monroe picked up the phone. Twenty minutes went by before he obtained the information. "It's an unlisted number in Clayton," he said, "registered in the name of Barto Sigor."

"Barto!" Joe exclaimed. "Mr Alden's chief sheet-metal worker!"

Mr Hardy jumped to his feet. "There's no time to lose!" he told his sons. "We're flying back to Bayport immediately!"

Shortly Jack Wayne and his passengers were airborne. When they reached their destination, the Hardys drove at once to Alden's plant. They found the executive in his office. He was greatly upset.

"What's wrong?" Frank asked.

"Barto drove off in my experimental car!" Alden declared.

"When?"

"A few minutes ago! I've already notified the police."

"Have you any idea which way he went?" Joe asked.

"No."

"Your car has a bright silver finish and a distinctive shape," Frank commented. "We should be able to spot it from the air."

"Good idea!" Mr Hardy said. "You boys go aloft. I'll stay here with Mr Alden in case the police come up with anything."

Frank rushed to the phone and dialled the number of Jack Wayne's office at the Bayport field. Luckily he caught the pilot just as he was about to go home.

"Sorry to ask you to go up again," he said. "You've been doing so much flying the past couple of days you're likely to sprout wings. But this is an emergency!"

"I don't mind," the pilot assured him.

Frank glanced at Alden. "Is it okay if Jack lands the

plane on your private drag strip?" he asked. "It'll save time."

"By all means," the executive said.

Soon the boys and their pilot were cruising high above the plant.

"Where do we start searching?" Joe inquired.

"My guess is that Barto will stick to the back roads," Frank explained. "There are lots of them to the west."

Jack manœuvred the sleek aircraft in a westerly direction. Frank and Joe scanned the terrain below. Thin ribbons of secluded roads cut across the hills and through the heavy forests.

"I'll climb a bit higher so that you can take in more area," the pilot said, as he advanced the throttle.

More minutes passed. Then suddenly Joe pointed down towards a bright speck moving along one of the narrow roads. "Look!" he cried. "That might be the car!"

"I'll go down on the deck and make a head-on pass," Jack announced.

Descending to almost ground level, the pilot headed towards the oncoming vehicle. The tall trees that flanked the road seemed just inches away from the wing tips.

"It's Mr Alden's racing car all right!" Frank observed. "Barto is pulling it off to the side."

The plane swept by the vehicle at high speed. Then Jack pulled up into a climbing turn and came round for a second pass. As he did this, Frank saw a man run out on to the road. "Must be Barto!" he shouted.

As Jack flew closer, the boys noticed that the man was aiming a long, cylindrical object at them.

"Be careful!" Frank warned the pilot. "It might be a weapon of some kind!"

In the next instant the windows of the plane crazed completely. The occupants were unable to see through the milky whiteness.

"We're flying blind!" Jack cried, as he hauled back on the control wheel and soared skywards.

"How can we land?" Frank asked tensely.

· 17 ·

Emergency Landing

THE Hardys sat frozen in their seats. They heard the loud, thudding sound of the treetops whipping against the underside of the wings.

"I veered off course slightly!" Jack cried. "We just managed to clear the trees!"

Seconds later a large, dark shadow flashed over the top of the plane's canopy. This was followed by a severe buffeting that rocked the craft violently.

"What was that?" Joe shouted.

"We almost collided with another plane!" the pilot declared nervously. "I must contact air traffic control. They'll have to handle us just as if we were flying in bad weather!"

Jack switched the radio transceiver to emergency frequency. "Mayday! Mayday! Mayday!" he declared. "Bayport Centre! Do you read me?"

There was an immediate reply as the radio's loudspeaker crackled to life. "This is Bayport Centre!" came a voice. "Aircraft calling Mayday! Give position, altitude, and identification!"

"This is Skyhawk One-One-Eight-Howe-Boscoe!" the pilot responded. "Now inbound on the two-eight-four-degree radial of Bayport Omni, approximately forty miles from the station! Present altitude, three thousand!" He then explained their predicament.

"Roger, Eight-Howe-Boscoe!" the air traffic operator replied. "Maintain present heading and altitude! Will advise when we have radar contact!"

It was several minutes before the air traffic controller informed Jack that the plane had been identified on the radar screens. He was also told that his craft would be brought down for a landing by means of a Ground Approach. Frank and Joe knew this meant radar operators would detect their aircraft's heading, descent, and distance from a landing runway. Jack Wayne would be literally "talked down".

The boys watched in admiration as he skilfully manœuvred the plane. When finally advised by the controller that he had just crossed the threshold of the runway, Jack chopped the power and settled to the ground.

"Whew!" Joe sighed, mopping his forehead. "I don't want to go through that again. For a while it was like driving in heavy traffic with your eyes shut."

Jack brought the plane to a stop. "We'll wait here until a tractor arrives to tow us back to the hangar."

After this was done, the Hardys and their pilot examined the windows of the plane curiously.

"I've never seen anything like it," Joe declared.

"It looks as if something had upset the molecular structure of the material in the windows," Jack said.

"Whatever caused the crazing," Frank concluded, must have had something to do with that gadget Barto was aiming at us."

"Let's search his apartment in Clayton," Joe suggested. "Maybe we'll find a clue."

"Just what I had in mind," Frank said. "I'll call Dad at Mr Alden's office and ask if he can arrange to get a search warrant."

"I almost forgot," Joe interjected. "Our car is at the plant."

"Use mine," Jack said, tossing a set of keys to the boys. "I'll stay here and see about getting the windows replaced."

The boys hurried off to meet their father at Alden's office.

"The warrant's all set," Mr Hardy said. "Clayton Police Station is sending a man to meet us at Barto's apartment."

They were greeted by a jolly, sturdily built policeman. "I got a master key from the superintendent," he informed them. "Makes it easier."

The Hardys were not surprised by what they saw when entering the apartment. A chest of drawers had been emptied of its contents and the closets were bare. The general untidiness of the rooms indiciated that the tenant had left in a hurry.

"Barto didn't waste any time getting out of here," Joe commented.

"Dodson's call from Haversville obviously scared him away," Frank concluded. "He knew the police might check his number."

"This proves one thing," Mr Hardy put in. "Barto must be in with the gang that's after Alden's motor. In fact, he might even be the leader."

Frank discovered a single fingerprint on the telephone. He lifted the print with his special tape and placed it in a celluloid container. "Must be Barto's," he remarked. "But I'll ask Chief Collig to check it just to be sure."

Meanwhile, Joe was rummaging through the wastebasket. He pulled out a crumpled, typewritten letter and two sheets of carbon paper. "I've found something," he called to his brother and father. They examined the letter together. It read:

Dear Barto:

I'm sorry to hear that your brother had trouble with his employer and moved on. Perhaps the strain of his labours was too much for him.

I wish you could visit me. I'm still operating my old mansion as a restaurant. One night I had forty customers. They came from miles around. However, I have competition about two miles north of my place. It is called the Claymore. Tonight I intend to go there to see how well they are doing. It is just off the main highway. I must go now, since it is getting late and I always make a point of retiring by twelve.

Write soon.

Your friend,
Eric

"I wonder who Eric is," Joe mused.

"Too bad we don't have the envelope the letter came in," Mr Hardy said. "It would tell us where it was mailed."

"What's written looks innocent enough," Frank observed. "Just the same, I want to examine it more carefully, and for luck I'll take these two sheets of carbon paper."

A further search of the rooms revealed nothing more. The Hardys thanked the Clayton policeman who had been assigned to accompany them and returned to Bayport. Frank stopped to give Chief Collig the fingerprint he had lifted from Barto's phone.

"I'll check it right away," the officer said.

"Thanks," Frank responded. "I'll be at home. Please call me there."

The boys and their father arrived home to find Aunt Gertrude in a jovial mood. "I have wonderful news!" she exclaimed. "Mr Benson telephoned. He's found a buyer. My stable is as good as sold."

"Glad to hear it," Mr Hardy told her. "That should put your mind at rest."

"Indeed it will," Aunt Gertrude agreed. "But I hope the new owner is an expert in caring for horses. I would dislike the thought of those poor animals being neglected."

"Do I detect a change of heart?" Joe asked, with a grin. "How come you're so fond of horses all of a sudden?"

"I always have been," Aunt Gertrude defended herself. "I just don't think they should be raced round a silly track for people's amusement."

Joe said, his eyes twinkling, "Someday I'm going to take you to a race!"

After supper the boys went to their crime lab and examined the letter they had found in Barto's apartment.

"Do you think it contains some kind of a code message?" Joe asked his brother.

"Not any more than the first letter I found in Barto's

wastebasket the day I took his fingerprints from the doorknob," Frank replied. "What about the sheets of carbon paper?"

"Haven't had a chance to examine them carefully yet," Joe said. "So far, it looks quite ordinary."

At that moment Chet Morton entered the lab. "Hi, master minds," he greeted the Hardys. "Got a few minutes to talk?"

"We always have time for you," Frank assured his friend, with a smile. "What's on your mind?"

"It's about my rocket cycle," Chet announced.

"Oh, no!" Joe exclaimed. "I thought you gave that up as a bad idea."

"I intended to," Chet replied. "But then I had a brainstorm."

Frank winked at his brother. "This ought to be good," he remarked.

"Okay!" Chet protested. "If you don't want to hear about my invention, just say so."

"I'm sorry," Frank said. "Go ahead."

The chubby youth took a rolled sheet of paper from his hip pocket and spread it out across the table. On it was the rough sketch of a bicycle. "See these tubes underneath the seat?" he began.

"Yes," Joe told him. "How could we forget? They're your rockets."

"Wrong!" Chet declared with a flourish of his hand. "What you see are jet engines. And I won't even have to build them myself. The hobby shop sells these units for model planes and boats. About four of them will produce enough thrust to propel my bike."

"If you insist on going ahead with the project,"

Frank warned, "just make sure that there are plenty of hedges around for you to fall into."

"Stow the comedy," Chet retorted. "The bike won't run away with me again. Since the jets are operated with liquid fuel, I'll be able to control the power."

"When do you plan to unveil this great invention of yours?" Joe inquired sceptically.

"In a couple of days," Chet announced proudly.

"This calls for a celebration," Frank said. "Aunt Gertrude baked an apple pie today. What say we go to the kitchen and have some?"

"Lead me to it!" their friend exclaimed.

As the boys were being served, Chief Collig telephoned. "I just got the results on the fingerprint you gave me," he said to Frank.

"I assume it's Barto's," Frank commented.

"No," the chief replied. "The print is from his brother Vilno!"

·18·

Night Chase

"THAT's incredible!" Frank declared.

He and Joe rushed to their father's study to tell him the news.

"Then Vilno was in his brother's apartment," Mr Hardy concluded. "But why?"

"To help Barto steal the experimental car," Joe suggested.

"If so," Frank argued, "why wasn't Vilno with his brother when we spotted the car from the air?"

"Maybe they decided to go their separate ways after the theft," Mr Hardy said.

Frank frowned. "I wonder," he muttered, "if Vilno has been posing as his brother all the time."

"Impossible!" Joe said. "Those were Barto's finger-prints you lifted off the doorknob the day you followed him to his apartment. And don't forget, Vilno is not a sheet-metal worker. How could he do his brother's job at the plant?"

"Guess you're right," Frank finally agreed. "But it's an interesting theory."

Mr Hardy rubbed his chin dubiously. "I'm going to try getting more background on those two," he said. "It may lead up a blind alley. Yet I might discover some useful information."

Their discussion was interrupted by a telephone call from Alden.

"The police have retrieved my experimental car," the executive told Mr Hardy. "Unfortunately Barto got away."

"What happened?" the detective asked.

Alden explained that a state trooper, who was patrolling the road indicated by the boys, had spotted the car travelling at great speed. He gave chase, but found that his motorcycle was not fast enough to close the gap.

"Then Barto blew a tyre and spun out of control," Alden continued. "By the time the officer reached the spot, Barto was gone."

"Was the car damaged?" Mr Hardy queried.

"A little," Alden answered. "But nothing that can't be repaired in a few hours. In fact, I had considered entering it in a road race that's scheduled near here a couple of days from now. However, I don't think I will."

After hanging up, the detective told his sons what Alden had said.

"I wonder where Barto was taking the car," Joe mused.

"Your guess is as good as mine," Mr Hardy admitted.

Frank thought for a moment. "I have an idea," he said finally. "Let's ask Mr Alden to enter his car in the road race. Then the night before the event Joe and I will inspect the route. We might spot one of those signposts."

"It's worth a try," their father agreed.

The following morning Frank telephoned Alden and told him his plan.

"I'll do anything to help clear up the mystery," Alden stated. He agreed to the plan, then described the route of the race.

After Frank put down the phone, Joe said, "I hope you don't plan on our using bicycles like the last time. If you do, I'm going to ask Chet to install a couple of his jet engines on mine."

Frank grinned. "We'll use our car."

"But if there are members of the gang around, they'll hear us coming," Joe objected.

"So far, the signposts have been set precisely beyond a sharp curve in the road. There'll be a full moon. We can cruise along with our lights out, and every time we come to a curve we'll stop and inspect it on foot."

It was clear and cool the night before the event. The boys waited until midnight before starting out for the race site, which was situated a few miles west of Clayton. When they arrived, Frank turned out the headlights and drove slowly along the route described by Alden.

"Maybe we're too early," Joe warned. "If the gang does intend putting up a signpost, we might finish our search before they get here."

"We'll keep patrolling the road till dawn," Frank said. "If they haven't set one up already, they'll have to do it before daylight."

The boys stared into the darkness. As they approached the first sharp bend in the road, Frank stopped the car. He and his brother edged their way around it on foot.

"Nothing there," Joe observed.

The Hardys returned to the car and continued on.

They had almost covered the entire route when another sharp bend appeared ahead of them. They climbed out of the vehicle and walked forward.

"Hold it!" Joe ordered in a low voice. "Do you hear something?"

Frank listened, then nodded. "Sounds like several men mumbling to one another," he whispered.

Crouching low, the boys cautiously worked their way around the bend. Then suddenly the Hardys came to a stop. The shadowy images of five men could be seen standing near a pickup truck a short distance down the road. A signpost stood nearby.

"Rotten luck," one of the men growled in a hushed voice. "This generator we brought doesn't work."

"We should've checked it out at the lab," another man added.

"I know those voices," Frank hissed. "It's Dodson and Barto!"

"I wonder if Vilno is with them," Joe whispered.

A couple of men lifted a heavy object on to the back of the truck.

"Slade! You and Tadlow go back and get another generator," Barto ordered. "But be quick about it. Everything has to be set up before it gets light."

Two men leaped into the truck and started off. The driver executed a U-turn and headed in the direction of the Hardys.

Frank pointed to a clump of brush a few feet away. "Take cover!"

The boys managed to conceal themselves just before the truck flashed by.

"They're bound to spot our car!" Joe said anxiously.

A moment later he and Frank were panic-stricken to hear the truck screech to a halt. Soon one of its occupants came running back to rejoin his companions.

"Barto!" the man exclaimed. "There's a car parked beyond the bend. It wasn't there before!"

"Maybe it's the police!" Dodson spluttered.

"I don't think so," Barto argued. "They would've driven up and asked us what we're doing here." He turned to his pals. "Spread out and start searching the area. There must be snoopers around."

The men took out flashlights and began walking down the road towards the Hardys.

"What'll we do?" Joe said.

"Our only chance is to make a break for it," Frank decided. "Head for the car. There'll be only one man to get past."

The boys leaped to their feet and sprinted down the road as fast as they could.

"Look!" Barto yelled, as he directed his beam of light towards the fleeing youths. "There go a couple of guys!"

"It's those Hardy kids!" Dodson shouted. "Don't let them get away!"

As Frank and Joe rounded the bend, they saw the driver of the truck standing beside their car. Joe crouched low, shot forward, and buried his right shoulder into the man's midriff. The fellow went crashing to the ground.

Frank leaped behind the steering wheel of the car and started the engine. Joe climbed in beside him just as Barto and his friends bore down on the boys.

"Stop them!" Dodson yelled.

"Don't let those Hardy kids get away!" shouted
Dodson

After making a quick U-turn, the boys sped along the road and away from their pursuers. Joe peered out of the rear window. "They're coming after us in the truck!"

Frank gave the convertible more power. "Are they gaining on us?"

"No!" Joe answered. "But we're not losing them either!"

After rounding another sharp bend in the road, Frank noticed a trail ahead which struck off to the right and into a wooded area. "Hang on!" he cried. "I'm going to try something!"

Swerving sharply, Frank turned on to the trail. After they had travelled a short distance, he switched off the engine and lights. A moment later their pursuers raced past and continued down the road.

"Your manœuvre worked!" Joe said with a grin.

"We're not out of this yet," Frank warned. "Barto and his men are sure to figure out what happened. We'll get back on the road and drive in the opposite direction."

He restarted the engine and rolled only a few feet when he brought the vehicle to a stop.

"What's wrong?" Joe queried.

"I'm afraid we have a flat!"

The boys climbed out of the car and were dismayed to see that the left front tyre had been punctured by a sharp rock.

"What a time to have this happen!" Joe muttered.

At that instant they heard the sound of a vehicle approaching in the distance.

"It must be Barto and the others!" Joe concluded.

"Quick! Let's hide!"

"Where?"

Frank glanced around. "We'll climb a tree. That one over there should be the easiest. Get going! I'll follow you!"

Soon the Hardys were pulling themselves up through the branches, high above the ground. A thick mass of leaves provided excellent cover. There was one small clear spot which permitted them to view the road.

"We made it just in time," Joe said. "There's the pickup truck. Barto and his men are turning in here!"

The boys' pulses quickened as they watched the truck come to a halt immediately behind their car.

"I told you those kids must've turned in here after we didn't see them on the road ahead!" Dodson declared. "Good trick. Lucky I remembered our passing this trail."

"But where are they?" Barto growled. He examined the damaged tyre. "I see they have a flat. Why didn't they try to fix it?"

"Probably heard us coming and ran off," Dodson replied. "Just the same, let's take a look around."

Frank and Joe were almost afraid to breathe as they watched their pursuers take out flashlights and search the area. At one point, a beam of light was directed towards the place in which the boys were hiding.

"That was close," Frank thought, as the beam was finally turned downwards.

"We'd better not waste any more time here!" Barto shouted. "Those snoopers may be on their way to call the police!"

"They've ruined everything," Dodson snarled.

"We'll have to forget about using the signpost on Alden's car during the race. Let's pick it up and get out of here."

One of the men walked to the rear of the Hardys' car with a sharp-pointed tool. He proceeded to punch several holes in the fuel tank. Gasoline began to stream from it. "That'll stop 'em from usin' this in case they come back."

Barto and his henchmen climbed into the truck and drove off. The Hardys waited for a few minutes before leaving their hiding place.

"Here we are in the middle of nowhere without transportation," Joe said angrily.

"Won't help to complain about it." Frank sighed. "Must be five or six miles to the nearest telephone. Let's start walking."

They began trekking along the road. It had been daylight for more than an hour when they saw a saloon car approaching.

"Oh-oh," Joe remarked. "I hope none of Barto's men are in it."

As the car came to a stop, the boys were elated to see Alden behind the wheel and their father seated beside him.

"Am I glad to see you two!" Mr Hardy called out. "I became worried when I didn't hear from you. I decided to look for you and asked Mr Alden to come along." He peered at his sons curiously. "Why are you walking? Where's your car?"

The boys climbed into the rear seat of Alden's car and told the men what had happened. Then they drove to the spot where they had seen the signpost.

"This is where it was," Frank announced, pointing to a small hole on the shoulder of the road.

"The gang made certain that they didn't leave any clues behind," Mr Hardy observed.

"You boys have saved my experimental car from being wrecked," Alden interjected.

"You must be tired," Mr Hardy said to his sons.

"I insist you come to my house for breakfast and a few hours' sleep," Alden added.

The young detectives readily agreed. They rested until mid-afternoon, then returned to Alden's office. They had been there for only a few minutes when the phone rang. Alden picked up the receiver. He turned pale as he listened to what his caller had to say.

"What's the matter?" Mr Hardy asked after his client hung up.

"That—that was Barto's brother Vilno!" Alden stammered. "He has Roger! He said unless I give him my experimental motor, he'll harm my son. He's calling again in two hours for my answer."

· 19 ·

Breaking the Code

THE Hardys were shocked by the news.

Alden was almost at the point of collapse. "If Vilno and his gang want my motor that badly, I'll give it to them."

The three detectives were angry. Mr Hardy exclaimed, "I'd like to get my hands on those scoundrels! They'll stop at nothing!"

"If only we had a lead to where their hideout is," Joe put in.

Frank frowned. "Maybe the lead is right in our files at home."

"What do you mean?" Joe asked.

"Maybe the letters we found in Barto's apartment do contain a code after all," Frank answered.

Mr Hardy nodded. "Why don't you boys go back to Bayport and work on that angle?" He handed them a set of keys. "Take my car. It's in the plant's car park. I'll stay here and be on hand when Vilno calls back."

"Meanwhile," Alden told the boys, "I'll send one of my tow trucks to pick up your car."

Frank and Joe hurried home, took Barto's letters from the file, then went to their crime lab to study them.

After an hour had passed, Joe sighed. "We're no closer to discovering a key than we were the last time we examined the letters."

"Looks hopeless," Frank agreed. "But let's keep at it a bit longer."

Shrugging, Joe turned his attention to the sheets of carbon paper found in Barto's apartment. He scrutinized them carefully and thought they looked a bit different from the usual carbon paper. Suspicious, Joe sandwiched a sheet between two sheets of white paper, picked up a pencil, and began scribbling on the upper one.

Suddenly he sat bolt upright. "This is odd! The carbon doesn't produce a copy except in a few isolated spots."

Frank jumped to his feet. "Joe! You may have discovered the key to the code!"

"I hope so. Fortunately our typewriter has pica type like Barto's machine. I'll type an exact copy of the first of his letters," Joe said. "If our hunch is correct . . ." His words trailed off as he inserted two clean sheets into the typewriter. Then he began tapping out the words.

Dear Eric:

Forgive me for taking so long to write you, but I've been so exhausted from work the last few days that I didn't feel I could write a coherent sentence. How I wish I had the stamina of two hard-working boys who have taken summer jobs at the plant. Any family would be proud to have sons like that.

As I already told you, my brother has left the Alden company . . .

When Joe finished typing the letter, he pulled out the sheets and quickly examined the carbon copy.

"That's it! We've broken the code!" he exclaimed. "Trick carbon paper!"

Joe showed Frank the copy. "Notice that the carbon has transferred only certain words and portions of words on to the copy sheet. First we have the word 'hard'. Next, the 'y' and 's' from the word 'boys'."

"Spelling out 'Hardys'!" Frank declared.

"And the next word is 'sons', and so on."

The boys observed that the complete message read:

Hardys, sons of detective, here. I'm sure they're investigating.

Tingling with excitement, Frank handed his brother the second of Barto's letters and the other sheet of carbon paper. "Quick! Make a copy of this!"

Joe repeated the procedure. The carbon copy revealed the following message:

moved lab to old mansion forty miles north of Clayton on route twelve.

"It must be the location of the gang's hideout!" Frank exclaimed.

He rushed to the telephone and dialled Alden's private office number. There was no answer.

"It's after office hours," Joe said. "Mr Alden's secretary must have left. Why don't you try the company's main number?"

Following his brother's suggestion, Frank finally got a response from the plant's chief watchman. "Sorry, I can't help you," the man told Frank. "Me and my men just came on duty. I haven't seen Mr Alden or anyone else."

Next, Frank tried the executive's home. Again there was no answer.

"I wonder where Dad and Mr Alden are," Frank muttered.

"Maybe they went to meet Vilno."

"Dad would have called us. I don't like this."

"If they're delivering the experimental motor to Vilno, he and his gang may try to make a getaway after they have it. Let's go to their hideout."

"Okay!" Frank agreed. "But since Mother and Aunt Gertrude won't get home from the theatre till late I'll ask Chet to stand by the phone here. He can tell Dad where we are if he should call."

Twenty minutes later Chet's ancient yellow car rumbled to a stop in front of the Hardy home. The boys noticed that their friend had his jet-propelled bicycle lashed to the rear bumper.

"I'm taking my bike to a secret spot early tomorrow morning," Chet announced. "It's ready for the supreme test."

"Lots of luck," Frank said. "I hope the job we're asking you to do isn't going to interfere with your plans."

"Not at all," the chubby youth replied grandly. "What is it you want me to tell your father if he calls?"

Frank handed him the message they had decoded revealing the location of the gang's hideout.

"I'd rather be going with you," Chet muttered, "instead of having to sit at the telephone."

"We wish you could too," Joe assured him. "But

your job is an important one. We'll check with you later."

It was already dusk when the Hardys drove off. Forty miles to the north of Clayton, Joe pointed to a dimly lighted building in the distance. "I think I've spotted the mansion! It's behind those trees over to the right."

Frank brought the car to a stop near the foot of a long wooded driveway. He and his brother continued on foot. The house was situated quite a distance from the main road.

"I don't see anybody or signs of activity," Joe whispered as they neared the building.

"Just the same, be careful. If this *is* Vilno's hideout he's sure to have one or more guards posted."

The boys crept forward towards the front of the house, keeping in the darkness of the trees. Suddenly Joe grabbed his brother's arm. "Look!" he whispered. "There's a man up ahead, seated on that big rock. He's armed!"

"It's a guard all right, Joe. He's Tadlow, one of the men we saw with Barto and Dodson at the sinister signpost!"

"Then we're at the right place. Let's nab him."

"Okay."

The Hardys stalked their quarry. When they were within arm's reach of the man, he jumped to his feet and whirled round to face them.

Quick as a flash Joe leaped and caught the man squarely on the jaw with a right uppercut. He tumbled to the ground unconscious. Nearby lay his rifle, which Frank flung into a clump of brush.

The boys dragged the man to a slim tree, put his arms around the trunk, and tied his wrists together with a belt. The placing of a handkerchief gag completed the job.

Moving cautiously, the boys continued towards the mansion. They kept a sharp lookout for other guards, but there were none. When the Hardys reached their goal, they detected a humming sound.

"What do you think that is?" Joe hissed.

"Offhand, I'd say it's some kind of machine," Frank answered. "Seems to be coming from the basement."

The boys started to creep round the outside of the mansion. Soon they discovered a metal air vent in the foundation. Frank peered through it in amazement.

"See anything?" Joe asked in a hushed voice.

"Yes. Looks like a physics or electronics laboratory."

Joe crouched just as three men came into Frank's view. They were Vilno, Barto, and Dodson. The boys pressed their ears against the vent in an effort to hear what the men were saying.

"This is a good set-up here," Barto remarked. "Too bad we have to leave it."

"Now that we have the experimental motor," Vilno put in, "there's no reason for us to stick around."

"What about the prisoners?" Dodson inquired. "Alden and his son don't worry me, but that detective Hardy can be dangerous to us."

Frank and Joe gasped. Their father had been captured together with Mr Alden and Roger!

"Forget it," Vilno told Dodson. "We'll be miles away before anyone finds Hardy."

Frank turned to his brother. "We must rescue them!"

"We can't do it alone! There are probably more members of the gang inside."

Suddenly the tall figure of a man loomed up behind the boys. "Who are you?" he demanded.

Frank and Joe leaped to defend themselves. A wild struggle followed. They crashed against the side of the house several times. Then Frank dealt the man a blow that sent him crumbling to the ground.

Suddenly the young detectives heard another, but louder, humming sound. In the next instant they were horror-stricken to find that they could not move.

"What's happening?" Joe exclaimed.

The boys were frozen in their tracks. Some powerful, invisible force was holding them!

·20·

Jet Action

"IT'S THE Hardy kids!" Dodson shouted as he, Barto, and two other men arrived on the scene.

"Don't get too close to them," Barto warned his pals, "or you'll get caught in the sonic trap yourselves. Tadlow! Go and tell my brother to turn it off."

Within a couple of minutes the boys were released from the mysterious force that had prevented them from moving. The after effects, however, caused Frank and Joe to fall to the ground, exhausted. Dodson and the others pounced on them and tied the boys' hands behind their backs.

"So! How do you like our little sonic trap?" Barto sneered.

"Sonic trap?" Frank said weakly.

"Yes," Barto replied. "It's another of Vilno's inventions. A device which encloses objects of our choosing within a solid shell of hypersonic vibrations. Your father also had the honour of experiencing its effects."

Frank and Joe were marched into the mansion, then down a flight of stairs leading to the basement. They were awed by what they saw. The area had been converted into a large laboratory, and was filled with various pieces of electronic equipment. In one corner of the room lay several signposts marked DANGER.

"Welcome! Welcome!" Vilno exclaimed with exaggerated politeness. "Looking for your father? Well, you've come to the right place."

"If you've harmed him," Joe began, "or . . ."

"He's perfectly fit," Vilno interrupted, "and is in our storage room with Alden and his son. You shall join them shortly."

For the first time the boys had an opportunity to see Vilno and Barto together. They were identical twins. Except for a difference in dress, it was difficult to tell who was who.

"Perhaps our guests would like to see some of the things we invented," Barto sneered.

"That *we* invented? You're forgetting it was my genius alone that made our devices possible!" his twin said boastfully.

"How did you manage to craze the windshields of Mr Alden's racing cars?" Frank interjected.

Vilno seemed pleased by the question. He led the Hardys to the signposts. "Inside each of these is a hypersonic generator of my own design. I found that I could disturb the molecular arrangement in some materials with the waves it produces. These are what crazed the windshields of Alden's cars."

"And the windows of our plane!" Joe said angrily.

"Ah yes," Vilno said. A sinister smile spread across his face. He walked to a table and picked up a long, cylindrical object. "Your plane was among the first objects on which I tried the portable version of the hypersonic generator."

"Then it was you, and not Barto, who stole Mr Alden's experimental car," Frank remarked.

"Precisely," Vilno replied.

At that moment Barto began to roar with laughter. "They still don't know," he told his brother, "that it was you who was working at the plant all the time, posing as me!"

"But how could you carry on the deception?" Joe spluttered. "You're not a sheet-metal worker."

"That's where you're wrong," Vilno shot back. "My brother and I were both trained in sheet-metal work as youths. But I never claimed it as one of my skills. My ambition was to become a scientist."

"Why are we standing around here talking?" Dodson said impatiently. "These snoopers might have told the police they were coming here!"

"Then where are they?" Vilno countered. "You worry too much."

"I don't care what you say!" Dodson retorted. "I . . ."

"Shut up!" Barto broke in. "We should've let you stay in jail for stealing Alden's race horse. Why did you do it? Aren't we paying you enough?"

"And your stupidity didn't end with the horse theft," Vilno added, with a touch of irritation. "You made the mistake of telephoning me at my apartment from Haversville Police Headquarters. Idiot! I knew the Hardys were bound to check the number."

Dodson grimaced but said, "You're not so smart. You started a fire in the experimental lab."

Frank broke in. "Vilno, you say you were posing as your brother all the time. Yet it was Barto's fingerprints

I found on the doorknob of your apartment the day I followed you home from the plant."

"Quite simple," Vilno answered proudly."Barto and I were dressed exactly alike and switched places in the lobby. It was he you saw enter the apartment."

"But how did you know you were going to be followed that day?" Joe asked quickly.

"Your taking summer jobs at the plant didn't fool us," Barto put in. "We knew you were probably investigating the Alden case. Vilno guessed that he would be a suspect, and that you would undoubtedly shadow him. So, each day, we wore similar clothes in the event we had to switch places. The plan paid off. You followed the wrong one on the street in Clayton. Vilno pretended a friend was a tramp and shoved him away."

"We've told them enough," Vilno growled. "Put them in the storage room with the others."

Dodson and two men marched Frank and Joe out of the laboratory and down a narrow passageway. They came to a stop in front of a heavy metal door. Dodson pulled it open.

"Inside!" he ordered.

The boys entered a small, windowless room made of stone. Before the door was closed, they saw their father, Alden, and Roger.

"Dad!" Joe exclaimed.

"I see you two also had some bad luck," the detective said remorsefully.

The metal door clanged shut and the Hardys and their companions were in total darkness.

"We were surprised to learn that you and Mr Alden

had been captured, Dad," Frank remarked grimly.

"I walked into Vilno's sonic trap," Mr Hardy explained.

"How did you find the gang's hideout?" Joe asked.

"After you left Mr Alden's office, I went to Clayton Police Station in Mr Alden's car to tell them about the situation, and to arrange for help in case we needed it. I planned to return to the plant in time for Vilno's telephone call. When I was driving back, I saw Mr Alden go by me from the opposite direction in a truck."

"Sorry about that." The executive sighed. "This is how it happened, boys. Vilno called me again shortly after your father left. He told me he'd been watching the plant and saw Mr Hardy drive off. Vilno was worried he was going to the police and demanded I deliver the experimental motor to him immediately. For Roger's sake, I had no choice."

"What happened then?" Frank asked.

"Vilno ordered me to bring the motor to the Bryant crossroads north of Clayton," Mr Alden replied. "There, two of his men jumped into the truck with me and told me to drive on. We came here to the mansion."

"I followed the truck," Mr Hardy interjected. "Too bad I didn't have my own car, or I would have contacted you boys by radio. And unfortunately I couldn't stop to use a telephone."

"You people wouldn't be in this mess if it wasn't for me," Roger muttered.

Frank began to grope around their enclosure, hoping for a way of escape. His father said, "The walls are solid, and you couldn't budge that metal door with a bulldozer."

"The room is completely sealed," Mr Alden added, "except for an air vent. Thank goodness for that."

"Air vent," Frank repeated, looking for it.

"It's near the ceiling," Mr Hardy said. "But if you're thinking of an escape route, it's too small for any of us to crawl through."

"Let me try," Joe urged. "I've managed to squeeze through some pretty small spaces before."

Mr Hardy guided his sons to the rear wall of the room. "The vent should be directly above this spot."

Frank hoisted his brother on to his shoulders. Joe ran one hand along the upper portion of the wall. "I've found it! The vent is covered with a metal grating." There was a momentary pause. "I think I can pull it loose."

Joe tugged the grating hard. Finally it broke free of the wall. "The opening is small, but I'm sure I can manage to get through. Boost me up higher."

Frank grabbed his brother's feet with both hands and shoved him upward. An instant later Joe was gone.

"Be careful, son," Mr Hardy called.

But Joe was not free yet. He was in an air duct. His arms stretched out in front of him, Joe forced his way through the narrow passageway. Minutes seemed like hours. Finally he was elated to find that the vent led directly outside the mansion.

Another grating, however, barred his way. He grasped the bars with both hands and shoved with all his strength. The grating loosened and dropped outside to the ground.

After climbing out of the vent, Joe scanned his surroundings. Several yards away he saw Vilno and his henchmen preparing to depart in Alden's truck.

Stealthily, the young detective stalked towards the front door of the mansion. Luckily it was unlocked. He raced inside and ran down to the storage room to free his companions.

"Quick! Vilno and his men are getting ready to leave!"

The three Hardys and their friends rushed outside. They were crestfallen to see that the truck had already pulled away.

"We'll never catch them!" Frank declared.

"Look!" Joe yelled. "What's that glow?"

His companions were startled to see a bright ball of light approaching the truck head-on. Just as a collision seemed imminent, the vehicle veered off the lane. This was followed by a loud crunching sound.

"What's that?" Alden shouted.

They detected a roar as the glow grew closer. Then it suddenly vanished. Seconds later Chet Morton coasted out of the darkness on his jet-propelled bicycle.

"Hi, fellows! Am I glad to see you!"

"Chet! What are you doing here?" Frank exclaimed.

"I began to worry when I didn't hear from you," the chubby youth explained. "So did your mother and aunt. I decided to see what was going on. My car ran out of fuel about a mile from here, so I came the rest of the way on my jet bike." His eyes widened. "By the way, I almost ran into a truck! What happened to it?"

The Hardys hurried to the spot where they had seen the vehicle veer off the lane. They found it tightly wedged between two stout trees. Vilno and his pals were desperately trying to open the doors but without success.

Just then a State Police car arrived on the scene. One of the troopers got out. "Did any of you see a wild kid on a bicycle?" he questioned. "We think it turned in here. Looked as if it was on fire."

"I'm the one," Chet admitted sheepishly.

"What were you trying to do?" the officer demanded. "You went by us as if you'd been shot out of a cannon." His attention was attracted by the disabled truck. "What happened here? Accident?"

Mr Hardy stepped forward. "Let me explain," he said.

After hearing the story, the officer radioed for additional men, then the troopers took Vilno and his henchmen into custody.

"We'd have escaped if it hadn't been for that crazy friend of yours and his bicycle," the gang leader growled.

"That's your hard luck!" Joe told him.

Mr Hardy said, "We know that specifications of Mr Alden's motor were leaking out of the plant. How did you manage it?"

Vilno's egotism caused him to forget his predicament for a moment. "Easy! Alden's machinists worked from plans recorded on film slides. I just roamed around the plant and photographed the projected pictures with a spy camera in my wrist watch. Other components I committed to memory and put them down on paper later."

Soon more troopers arrived. The prisoners were herded into patrol cars. The case of *The Sinister Signpost*

158 THE SINISTER SIGNPOST

was over. Frank and Joe always regretted such a moment. They were not restless for long, however, because the mystery of the *Footprints Under the Window* soon came their way.

Before departing, one of the officers walked up to Chet. "I should give you a ticket for speeding," he announced, winking at the Hardys.

"I—I wish you wouldn't," Chet stammered. "It won't happen again."

"Well, under the circumstances, I think I can overlook it this time." The trooper sighed, trying not to grin. "Anyway, I wouldn't know how to describe your jet-propelled bike to the judge."

"We warned you about that invention of yours," Joe whispered, nudging his chum. "Lucky for us you didn't listen!"

The Three Investigators
Series

Meet the Three Investigators – brilliant Jupiter Jones, athletic Pete Crenshaw and studious Bob Andrews. Their motto, "We investigate anything" has led them into some bizarre and dangerous situations. Join the three boys in their sensational mysteries, available only in Armada.

ARMADA

The Hardy Boys Mystery Stories

ARMADA